The Library
of
Indiana Classics

The Bears
of
Blue River

BY

CHARLES MAJOR

Indiana University Press
Bloomington

First Midland Book Edition 1984

The Library of Indiana Classics is available in a special clothbound
library-quality edition and in a paperback edition.

Library of Congress Cataloging in Publication Data

Major, Charles, 1856–1913.
The bears of Blue River.
(The Library of Indiana classics)
Summary: Little Balser, a pioneer boy growing up in
early nineteenth-century Indiana, has many adventures
and dangerous encounters with bears while learning the
ways of the woods.
1. Indiana—History—Fiction. [1. Frontier and
pioneer life—Indiana—Fiction. 2. Indiana—Fiction.
3. Bears—Fiction] I. Title. II. Series.
PS2359.M648B4 1984 813'.4 83–49522
ISBN 0–253–10590–0
ISBN 0–253–20330–9 (pbk.)
8 9 10 99 98

CONTENTS.

CHAPTER VIII.

CHAPTER IX.

CHAPTER X.

THE BEARS OF BLUE RIVER.

I

THE BIG BEAR.

THE BEARS OF BLUE RIVER.

CHAPTER I.

THE BIG BEAR.

Away back in the "twenties," when Indiana was a baby state, and great forests of tall trees and tangled underbrush darkened what are now her bright plains and sunny hills, there stood upon the east bank of Big Blue River, a mile or two north of the point where that stream crosses the Michigan road, a cozy log cabin of two rooms — one front and one back.

The house faced the west and stretching off toward the river for a distance equal to twice the width of an ordinary street, was a blue-grass lawn, upon which stood a dozen or more elm and sycamore trees, with a few honey-locusts scattered here and there. Immediately at the water's edge was a steep slope of ten or twelve feet. Back of the house, mile upon mile, stretched the deep dark forest, inhabited by deer and bears, wolves and wildcats, squirrels and birds, without number.

In the river the fish were so numerous that they seemed to entreat the boys to

BASS AND SUNFISH AND THE BIG-MOUTHED REDEYE.

catch them, and to take them out of their crowded quarters. There were bass and black suckers, sunfish and catfish, to say nothing of the sweetest of all, the big-mouthed redeye.

South of the house stood a log barn, with room in it for three horses and two cows; and enclosing this barn, together with a piece

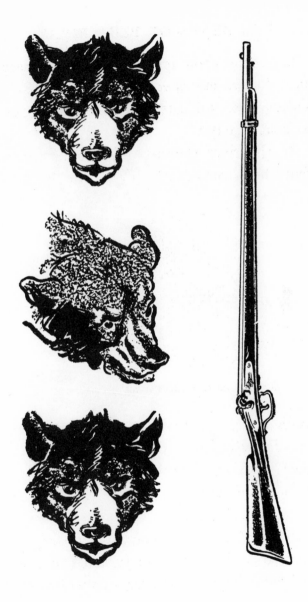

of ground, five or six acres in extent, was a palisade fence, eight or ten feet high, made by driving poles into the ground close to-gether.   In this enclosure the farmer kept his stock, consisting of a few sheep and cattle, and here also the chickens, geese, and ducks were driven at nightfall to save them from "varmints," as all prowling animals were called by the settlers.

The man who had built this log hut, and who lived in it and owned the adjoining land at the time of which I write, bore the name of Balser Brent. " Balser " is probably a cor-ruption of Baltzer, but, however that may be, Balser was his name, and Balser was also the name of his boy, who was the hero of the bear stories which I am about to tell you.

Mr. Brent and his young wife had moved to the Blue River settlement from North Carolina, when young Balser was a little boy five or six years of age. They had pur-chased the "eighty" upon which they lived, from the United States, at a sale of public land held in the town of Brookville on

Whitewater, and had paid for it what was then considered a good round sum — one dollar per acre. They had received a deed for their "eighty" from no less a person than James Monroe, then President of the United States. This deed, which is called a patent, was written on sheepskin, signed by the President's own hand, and is still preserved by the descendants of Mr. Brent as one of the title-deeds to the land it conveyed. The house, as I have told you, consisted of two large rooms, or buildings, separated by a passageway six or eight feet broad which was roofed over, but open at both ends — on the north and south. The back room was the kitchen, and the front room was parlour, bedroom, sitting room and library all in one.

At the time when my story opens Little Balser, as he was called to distinguish him from his father, was thirteen or fourteen years of age, and was the happy possessor of a younger brother, Jim, aged nine, and a little sister one year old, of whom he was very proud indeed.

On the south side of the front room was a large fireplace. The chimney was built of sticks, thickly covered with clay. The fireplace was almost as large as a small room in one of our cramped modern houses, and was broad and deep enough to take in backlogs which were so large and heavy that they could not be lifted, but were drawn in at the door and rolled over the floor to the fireplace.

The prudent father usually kept two extra backlogs, one on each side of the fireplace, ready to be rolled in as the blaze died down; and on these logs the children would sit at night, with a rough slate made from a flat stone, and do their "ciphering," as the study of arithmetic was then called. The fire usually furnished all the light they had, for candles and "dips," being expensive luxuries, were used only when company was present.

The fire, however, gave sufficient light, and its blaze upon a cold night extended halfway up the chimney, sending a ruddy, cozy glow to every nook and corner of the room.

The back room was the storehouse and kitchen; and from the beams and along the walls hung rich hams and juicy side-meat, jerked venison, dried apples, onions, and other provisions for the winter. There was a glorious fireplace in this room also, and a crane upon which to hang pots and cooking utensils.

The floor of the front room was made of logs split in halves with the flat, hewn side up; but the floor of the kitchen was of clay, packed hard and smooth.

The settlers had no stoves, but did their cooking in round pots called Dutch ovens. They roasted their meats on a spit or steel bar like the ramrod of a gun. The spit was kept turning before the fire, presenting first one side of the meat and then the other, until it was thoroughly cooked. Turning the spit was the children's work.

South of the palisade enclosing the barn was the clearing — a tract of twenty or thirty acres of land, from which Mr. Brent had cut and burned the trees. On this clearing the stumps stood thick as the hair on an angry dog's back; but the hard-working farmer ploughed between and around them, and each year raised upon the fertile soil enough wheat and corn to supply the wants of his family and his stock, and still had a little grain left to take to Brookville, sixty miles away, where he had bought his land, there to exchange for such necessities of life as could not be grown upon the farm or found in the forests.

The daily food of the family all came from the farm, the forest, or the creek. Their sugar was obtained from the sap of the sugar-trees; their meat was supplied in the greatest abundance by a few hogs, and by the inexhaustible game of which the forests were full. In the woods were found deer just for the shooting; and squirrels, rabbits, wild turkeys, pheasants, and quails, so numerous that a few hours' hunting would supply the table for days. The fish in the river, as I told you, fairly longed to be caught.

One day Mrs. Brent took down the dinner horn and blew upon it two strong blasts. This was a signal that Little Balser, who was helping his father down in the clearing, should come to the house. Balser was glad enough to drop his hoe and to run home. When he reached the house his mother said: —

"Balser, go up to the drift and catch a mess of fish for dinner. Your father is tired of deer meat three times a day, and I know he would like a nice dish of fried redeyes at noon."

"All right, mother," said Balser. And he immediately took down his fishing-pole and line, and got the spade to dig bait. When he had collected a small gourdful of angle-worms, his mother called to him: —

"You had better take a gun. You may meet a bear; your father loaded the gun this morning, and you must be careful in handling it."

Balser took the gun, which was a heavy rifle considerably longer than himself, and started up the river toward the drift, about a quarter of a mile away.

There had been rain during the night and the ground near the drift was soft.

Here, Little Balser noticed fresh bear tracks, and his breath began to come quickly. You may be sure he peered closely into every dark thicket, and looked behind all the large trees and logs, and had his eyes wide open lest perchance " Mr. Bear " should step out and surprise him with an affection-ate hug, and thereby put an end to Little Balser forever.

So he walked on cautiously, and, if the truth must be told, somewhat tremblingly, until he reached the drift.

Balser was but a little fellow, yet the stern necessities of a settler's life had compelled his father to teach him the use of a gun; and although Balser had never killed a bear, he had shot several deer, and upon one occasion had killed a wildcat, "almost as big as a cow," he said.

I have no doubt the wildcat seemed

"almost as big as a cow" to Balser when he killed it, for it must have frightened him greatly, as wildcats were sometimes dangerous animals for children to encounter.

"A WILDCAT ALMOST AS BIG AS A COW."

Although Balser had never met a bear face to face and alone, yet he felt, and many a time had said, that there wasn't a bear in the world big enough to frighten him, if he but had his gun.

He had often imagined and minutely detailed to his parents and little brother just what he would do if he should meet a bear. He would wait calmly and quietly until his bearship should come within a few yards of him, and then he would slowly lift his gun.

"LITTLE BALSER NOTICED FRESH BEAR TRACKS, AND HIS
BREATH BEGAN TO COME QUICKLY."

Bang! and Mr. Bear would be dead with a bullet in his heart.

But when he saw the fresh bear tracks, and began to realize that he would probably have an opportunity to put his theories about bear killing into practice, he began to wonder if, after all, he would become frightened and miss his aim. Then he thought of how the bear, in that case, would be calm and deliberate, and would put *his* theories into practice by walking very

"FRESH BEAR TRACKS."

politely up to him, and making a very satisfactory dinner of a certain boy whom he could name. But as he walked on and no bear appeared, his courage grew stronger as the prospect of meeting the enemy grew less, and he again began saying to himself that no bear could frighten him, because he had his gun and he could and would kill it.

So Balser reached the drift; and having looked carefully about him, leaned his gun against a tree, unwound his fishing-line from the pole, and walked out to the end of a log which extended into the river some twenty or thirty feet.

Here he threw in his line, and soon was so busily engaged drawing out sunfish and redeyes, and now and then a bass, which was hungry enough to bite at a worm, that all thought of the bear went out of his mind.

After he had caught enough fish for a sumptuous dinner he bethought him of going home, and as he turned toward the shore, imagine, if you can, his consternation when he saw upon the bank, quietly watching him, a huge black bear.

If the wildcat had seemed as large as a cow to Balser, of what size do you suppose that bear appeared? A cow! An elephant, surely, was small compared with the huge black fellow standing upon the bank.

It is true Balser had never seen an ele-phant, but his father had, and so had his

"IMAGINE . . HIS CONSTERNATION WHEN HE SAW UPON THE BANK, QUIETLY WATCHING HIM, A HUGE
BLACK BEAR."

friend Tom Fox, who lived down the **river**; and they all agreed that an elephant **was** "purt nigh as big as all outdoors."

The bear had a peculiar, determined expression about him that seemed to say: —

"That boy can't get away; he's out on the log where the water is deep, and if he

"THE BEAR HAD A PECULIAR, DETERMINED EXPRESSION ABOUT HIM."

jumps into the river I can easily jump in after him and catch him before he can swim a dozen strokes. He'll *have* to come off the log in a short time, and then I'll proceed to devour him."

About the same train of thought had also been rapidly passing through Balser's mind. His gun was on the bank where he had left it, and in order to reach it he would have to pass the bear. He dared not jump into the water, for any attempt to escape on his part would bring the bear upon him instantly. He was very much frightened, but, after all, was a cool-headed little fellow for his age; so he concluded that he would not press matters, as the bear did not seem inclined to do so, but so long as the bear remained watching him on the bank would stay upon the log where he was, and allow the enemy to eye him to his heart's content.

There they stood, the boy and the bear, each eying the other as though they were the best of friends, and would like to eat each other, which, in fact, was literally true.

Time sped very slowly for one of them, you may be sure; and it seemed to Balser that he had been standing almost an age in the middle of Blue River on that wretched shaking log, when he heard his mother's dinner horn, reminding him that it was time to go home.

Balser quite agreed with his mother, and gladly would he have gone, I need not tell you; but there stood the bear, patient, determined, and fierce; and Little Balser soon was convinced in his own mind that his time had come to die.

He hoped that when his father should go home to dinner and find him still absent, he would come up the river in search of him, and frighten away the bear. Hardly had this hope sprung up in his mind, when it seemed that the same thought had also occurred to the bear, for he began to move down toward the shore end of the log upon which Balser was standing.

Slowly came the bear until he reached the end of the log, which for a moment he examined suspiciously, and then, to Balser's great alarm, cautiously stepped out upon it and began to walk toward him.

Balser thought of the folks at home, and, above all, of his baby sister; and when he felt that he should never see them again, and that they would in all probability never know of his fate, he began to grow heavy hearted and was almost paralyzed with fear.

On came the bear, putting one great paw in front of the other, and watching Balser intently with his little black eyes. His tongue hung out, and his great red mouth was open to its widest, showing the sharp. long, glittering teeth that would soon be feasting on a first-class boy dinner.

When the bear got within a few feet of Balser — so close he could almost feel the animal's hot breath as it slowly approached — the boy grew desperate with fear, and struck at the bear with the only weapon he had — his string of fish.

Now, bears love fish and blackberries above all other food; so when Balser's string of fish struck the bear in the mouth, he grabbed at them, and in doing so lost his foothold on the slippery log and fell into the water with a great splash and plunge.

This was Balser's chance for life, so he flung the fish to the bear, and ran for the bank with a speed worthy of the cause.

"WHEN THE BEAR GOT WITHIN A FEW FEET OF BALSER . . . THE BOY GREW DESPERATE WITH FEAR, AND STRUCK AT THE BEAST WITH THE ONLY WEAPON HE HAD — HIS STRING OF FISH."

When he reached the bank his self-confidence returned, and he remembered all the things he had said he would do if he should meet a bear.

The bear had caught the fish, and again had climbed upon the log, where he was deliberately devouring them.

This was Little Balser's chance for death — to the bear. Quickly snatching up the gun, he rested it in the fork of a small tree near by, took deliberate aim at the bear, which was not five yards away, and shot him through the heart. The bear dropped into the water dead, and floated downstream a little way, where he lodged at a ripple a short distance below.

Balser, after he had killed the bear, became more frightened than he had been at any time during the adventure, and ran home screaming. That afternoon his father went to the scene of battle and took the bear out of the water. It was very fat and large, and weighed, so Mr. Brent said, over six hundred pounds.

Balser was firmly of the opinion that he himself was also very fat and large, and weighed at least as much as the bear. He was certainly entitled to feel "big"; for he had got himself out of an ugly scrape in a brave, manly, and cool-headed manner, and had achieved a victory of which a man might have been proud.

The news of Balser's adventure soon spread among the neighbours and he became quite a hero; for the bear he had killed was one of the largest that had ever been seen in that neighbourhood, and, besides the gallons of rich bear oil it yielded, there were three or four hundred pounds of bear meat; and no other food is more strengthening for winter diet.

There was also the soft, furry skin, which Balser's mother tanned, and with it made a coverlid for Balser's bed, under which he and his little brother lay many a cold night, cozy and "snug as a bug in a rug."

"THE BEAR HAD CAUGHT THE FISH AND AGAIN HAD CLIMBED UPON THE LOG"

CHAPTER II.

HOW BALSER GOT A GUN.

For many years after the killing of the big bear, as told in the preceding chapter, time was reckoned by Balser as beginning with that event. It was, if I may say it, his "Anno Domini." In speaking of occurrences, events, and dates, he always fixed them in a general way by saying, "That happened before I killed the big bear;" or, "That took place after I killed the big bear." The great immeasurable eternity of time was divided into two parts: that large unoccupied portion preceding the death of the big bear, and the part, full to overflowing with satisfaction and pride, after that momentous event.

Balser's adventure had raised him vastly in the estimation of his friends and neigh-bours, and, what was quite as good, had increased his respect for himself, and had given him confidence, which is one of the most valuable qualities for boy or man. Frequently when Balser met strangers, and the story of the big bear was told, they would pat the boy on the shoulder and call him a little man, and would sometimes ask him if he owned a gun. Much to Balser's sorrow, he was compelled to admit that he did not. The questions as to whether or not he owned a gun had put into his mind the thought of how delightful life would be if he but possessed one ; and his favourite visions by day and his sweetest dreams by night were all about a gun ; one not so long nor so heavy as his father's, but of the shorter, lighter pattern known as a smooth-bore carbine. He had heard his father speak of this gun, and of its effectiveness at short range ; and although at long distances it was not so true of aim as his father's gun, still he felt confident that, if he but possessed the coveted carbine he could, single-handed and alone, exterminate all the races of bears,

wolves and wildcats that inhabited the forests round about, and "pestered" the farmers
with their depredations.

But how to get the gun! That was the
question. Balser's father had received a gun
as a present from *his* father when Balser Sr.
had reached the advanced age of twenty-one,
and it was considered a rich gift. The cost
of a gun for Balser would equal half of the
sum total that his father could make during
an entire year; and, although Little Balser
looked forward in fond expectation to the
time when he should be twenty-one and
should receive a gun from his father, yet he
did not even hope that he would have one
before then, however much he might dream
about it. Dreams cost nothing, and guns
were expensive; too expensive even to be
hoped for. So Balser contented himself
with inexpensive dreams, and was willing,
though not content, to wait.

But the unexpected usually happens, at
an unexpected time, and in an unexpected
manner.

About the beginning of the summer after the killing of the big bear, when Balser's father had "laid by" his corn, and the little patch of wheat had just begun to take on a golden brown as due notice that it was nearly ready to be harvested, there came a few days of idleness for the busy farmer. Upon one of those rare idle days Mr. Brent and Balser went down the river on a fishing and hunting expedition. There was but one gun in the family, therefore Balser could not hunt when his father was with him, so he took his fishing-rod, and did great execution among the finny tribe, while his father watched along the river for game, as it came down to drink.

Upon the day mentioned Balser and his father had wandered down the river as far as the Michigan road, and Mr. Brent had left the boy near the road fishing, after telling him to go home in an hour or two, and that he, Mr. Brent, would go by another route and be home in time for supper.

So Balser was left by himself, fishing at a

deep hole perhaps a hundred yards north of the road. This was at a time when the river was in flood, and the ford where travellers usually crossed was too deep for passage.

Balser had been fishing for an hour or more, and had concluded to go home, when he saw approaching along the road from the east a man and woman on horseback. They soon reached the ford and stopped, believing it to be impassable. They were mud-stained and travel-worn, and their horses, covered with froth, were panting as if they had been urged to their greatest speed. After a little time the gentleman saw Balser, and called to him. The boy immediately went to the travellers, and the gentleman said: —

" My little man, can you tell me if it is safe to attempt the ford at this time ? "

" It will swim your horses," answered Balser.

" I knew it would," said the lady, in evident distress. She was young and pretty, and seemed to be greatly fatigued and frightened. The gentleman was very attentive and tried to soothe her, but in a moment or two she began to weep, and said : —

"They will catch us, I know.   They will catch us.   They cannot be more than a mile behind us now, and we have no place to turn."

"Is some one trying to catch you?" asked Balser.

The gentleman looked down at the little fellow for a moment, and was struck by his bright, manly air.   The thought occurred to him that Balser might suspect them of being fugitives from justice, so he explained : —

"Yes, my little fellow, a gentleman is trying to catch us.   He is this lady's father. He has with him a dozen men, and if they overtake us they will certainly kill me and take this lady home.   Do you know of any place where we may hide?"

"Yes, sir," answered Balser, quickly; "help me on behind you, and I'll take you to my father's house.   There's no path up the river, and if they attempt to follow they'll get lost in the woods."

Balser climbed on the horse behind the

gentleman, and soon they plunged into the deep forest, and rode up the river toward Balser's home. The boy knew the forest well, and in a short time the little party of three was standing at the hospitable cabin door. Matters were soon explained to Balser's mother, and she, with true hospitality, welcomed the travellers to her home. During the conversation Balser learned that the gentleman and lady were running away that they might be married, and, hoping to finish a good job, the boy volunteered the advice that they should be married that same evening under his father's roof. He also offered to go in quest of a preacher who made his home some two miles to the east.

The advice and the offer of services were eagerly accepted, and the lady and gentleman were married that night, and remained a few days at the home of Mr. Brent until the river was low enough to cross.

The strangers felt grateful to the boy who had given them such timely help, and asked him what they could do for him in return

Balser hesitated a moment, and said "There's only one thing I want very bad, but that would cost so much there's no use to speak of it."

"What is it, Balser? Speak up, and if it is anything I can buy, you shall have it."

"A gun! A gun! A smooth-bore carbine. I'd rather have it than anything else in the world."

"You shall have it if there's one to be bought in Indianapolis. We are going there, and will return within a week or ten days, and you shall have your carbine if I can find one."

Within two weeks after this conversation Balser was the happiest boy in Indiana, for he owned a carbine, ten pounds of fine powder, and lead enough to kill every living creature within a radius of five miles.

Of course the carbine had to be tested at once. So the day after he received it Balser started out with his father on a hunting expedition, fully determined in his own mind to kill a bear twice as large as his first one.

They took with them corn-bread and dried venison for dinner, and started east toward Conn's Creek, where the houses of the settlers were thinly scattered and game plentiful.

They had with them two faithful dogs, "Tige" and "Prince." Balser considered these dogs the most intelligent animals that walked on four feet. They were deer-hounds with a cross of bulldog, and were swift of foot and very strong.

Our hunters had travelled perhaps three or four miles into the forest when they started a deer, in pursuit of which the dogs bounded off with their peculiar bark, and soon deer and dogs were lost to sight. Balser and his father listened carefully for the voices of the dogs, for should the deer turn at bay, the dogs, instead of the quick bark, to which they gave voice in the chase, would utter a long-drawn-out note — half howl, half yelp.

The bay of the hounds had died away in the distance, and Balser and his father had heard nothing of them for two or three hours.

The hunters had seen other deer as they walked along, but they had been unable to obtain a shot. Smaller game was plentiful, but Balser and his father did not care to frighten away large game by shooting at squirrels or birds. So they continued their walk until they reached the bank of Conn's Creek, near the hour of noon; by that time Balser's appetite was beginning to call loudly for dinner, and he could not resist the temptation to shoot a squirrel, which he saw upon a limb of a neighbouring tree. The squirrel fell to the ground and was soon skinned and cleaned. Balser then kindled a fire, and cutting several green twigs, sharpened the ends and fastened small pieces of the squirrel upon them. He next stuck the twigs in the ground so that they leaned toward the fire, with the meat hanging directly over the blaze. Soon the squirrel was roasted to a delicious brown, and then Balser served dinner to his father, who was sitting on a rock near by. The squirrel, the corn-bread, and the venison quickly disappeared, and Balser, if permitted to do so, would have found another squirrel and would have cooked it.   Just as dinner was finished, there came from a long way up-stream the howling bark of Tige and Prince, telling, plainly as if they had spoken English, that the deer was at bay.

Thereupon Balser quickly loaded his gun, and he and his father looked carefully to their primings.   Then Mr. Brent directed Balser to climb down the cliff and move toward the dogs through the thicket in the bottom, while he went by another route, along the bluff.   Should the hunters be separated, they were to meet at an agreed place in the forest.   Balser climbed cautiously down the cliff and was soon deep in a dark thicket of tangled underbrush near the creek.

Now and then the deep bay of the dogs reached his ears from the direction whence he had first heard it, and he walked as rapidly as the tangled briers and under-growth would permit toward his faithful fellow-hunters.

He was so intent on the game which he knew the dogs held at bay, that he did not look about him with his accustomed caution, and the result of his unwatchfulness was that he found himself within ten feet of two huge bears before he was at all aware of their presence. They were evidently male and female, and upon seeing him the great he-bear gave forth a growl that frightened Balser to the depths of his soul. Retreat seemed almost impossible; and should he fire at one of the bears, his gun would be empty and he would be at the mercy of the other. To attempt to outrun a bear, even on level ground, would be almost a hopeless undertaking; for the bear, though an awkward-looking creature, is capable of great speed when it comes to a foot-race. But there, where the tangled underbrush was so dense that even walking through it was a matter of great difficulty, running was out of the question, for the thicket which would greatly impede Balser would be but small hindrance to the bears.

After Balser had killed the big bear at the drift, he felt that he never again would suffer from what hunters call "buck ager"; but when he found himself confronted by those black monsters, he began to tremble in every limb, and for the life of him could not at first lift his gun.   The he-bear was the first to move.   He raised himself on his haunches, and with a deep growl started for poor Balser.   Balser should have shot the bear as he came toward him, but acting solely from an instinct of self-preservation he started to run.   He made better headway than he had thought possible, and soon came to a small open space of ground where the undergrowth was not so thick, and where the bright light of the sun dispelled the darkness.   The light restored Balser's confidence, and the few moments of retreat gave him time to think and to pull himself to- gether.   So, turning quickly, he lifted his gun to his shoulder and fired at the bear, which was not two yards behind him.   Un- fortunately, his aim was unsteady, and his shot wounded the bear in the neck, but did not kill him.

Balser saw the disastrous failure he had made, and felt that the bear would be much surer in his attack upon him than he had been in his attack upon the bear. The boy then threw away his gun, and again began a hasty retreat.

He called for his father, and cried, " Tige! Prince! Tige! Tige!" not so much with a hope that either the dogs or his father would hear, but because he knew not what else to do. Balser ran as fast as he could, still the bear was at his heels, and the frightened boy expected every moment to feel a stroke from the brute's huge rough paw. Soon it came, with a stunning force that threw Balser to the ground, upon his back. The bear was over him in an instant, and caught his left arm between his mighty jaws. It seemed then that the light of the world went out for a moment, and he remembered nothing but the huge, blood-red mouth of the bear, his hot breath almost burning his cheeks, and his deep, terrible growls nearly deafening his ears. Balser's whole past life came up before him like a picture, and he remembered everything that had ever happened to him. He thought of how deeply his dear father and mother would grieve, and for the only time in his life regretted having received the carbine, for it was the gun, after all, that had got him into this trouble. All this happened in less time than it takes you to read ten lines of this page, but it seemed very, very long to Balser, lying there with the huge body of the bear over him.

Suddenly a note of hope struck his ear — the sweetest sound he had ever heard. It was the yelp of dear old Tige, who had heard his call and had come to the rescue. If there is any creature on earth that a bear thoroughly hates, it is a dog. Tige wasted not a moment's time, but was soon biting and pulling at the bear's hind legs. The bear immediately turned upon the dog, and gave Balser an opportunity to rise. Of this opportunity he quickly took advantage, you

may be sure.   Soon Prince came up also,
and in these two strong dogs the bear had
foemen worthy of his steel.

Balser's great danger and narrow escape
had quickened all his faculties, so he at once
ran back to the place where he had dropped
his gun, and although his left arm had been
terribly bitten, he succeeded in loading, and
soon came back to the help of the dogs, who
had given him such timely assistance.

The fight between the dogs and the bear
was going on at a merry rate, when Balser
returned to the scene of action.   With Prince
on one side and Tige on the other, both so
strong and savage, and each quick and nim-
ble as a cat, the bear had all he could do to
defend himself, and continually turned first
one way and then another in his effort to
keep their fangs away from his legs or throat.
This enabled Balser to approach within a
short distance of the bear, which he cautiously did.   Taking care not to wound
either of his faithful friends, he was more
fortunate in his aim than he had been the

first time, and gave the bear a mortal
wound.

The wounded animal made a hasty re·
treat back into the thicket, followed closely
by the dogs; but Balser had seen more than
enough of bear society in the thicket, and
prudently concluded not to follow.   He then
loaded his gun with a heavy charge of
powder only, and fired it to attract his
father's attention.   This he repeated several
times, until at last he saw the welcome form
of his father hurrying toward him from the
bluff.   When his father reached him and
saw that he had been wounded, Mr. Brent
was naturally greatly troubled; but Balser
said: "I'll tell you all about it soon.   Let's
go in after the bears.   Two of them are in
the thicket up there next to the cliff, and
the dogs have followed them.   If Tige had
not come up just in time, one of the bears
would have killed me; but I think the shot
I gave him must have killed him by this
time."

So without another word, Balser having

loaded his gun, they started into the dark thicket toward the cliff, in the direction whence came the voices of the dogs.

They had not proceeded farther than a hundred yards when they found the bear which Balser had shot, lying dead in the path over which Balser had so recently made his desperate retreat. The dogs were farther in, toward the cliff, where the vines, trees, and brush grew so thick that it was almost dark.

The two hunters, however, did not stop, but hurried on to the help of their dogs. Soon they saw through the gloom of the thicket the she-bear, and about her the dogs were prancing, barking, and snapping most furiously.

Carefully Balser and his father took their position within a few yards of the bear, and Balser, upon a signal from his father, called off the dogs so that a shot might be made at the bear without danger of killing either Tige or Prince.

Soon the report of two guns echoed

through the forest, almost at the same instant, and the great she-bear fell over on
her side, quivered for a moment, and died.
This last battle took place close by the stone
cliff, which rose from the bottom-land to a
height of fifty or sixty feet.

Balser and his father soon worked their
way through the underbrush to where the
she-bear lay dead. After having examined
the bear, Balser's attention was attracted to
a small opening in the cliff, evidently the
mouth of a cave which had probably been
the home of the bear family that he and his
father had just exterminated. The she-bear
had taken her stand at the door of her home,
and in defending it had lost her life. Balser
examined the opening in the cliff, and concluded to enter; but his father said: —

"You don't know what's in there. Let's
first send in one of the dogs."

So Tige was called and told to go into the
cave. Immediately after he had entered he
gave forth a series of sharp yelps which told
plainly enough that he had found something

worth barking at. Then Balser called the dog out, and Mr. Brent collected pieces of dry wood, and made a fire in front of the cave, hoping to drive out any animal that might be on the inside.

He more than suspected that he would find a pair of cubs.

As the smoke brought nothing forth, he concluded to enter the cave himself and learn what was there.

Dropping upon his knees, he began to crawl in at the narrow opening, and the boy and the two dogs followed closely. Mr. Brent had taken with him a lighted torch, and when he had gone but a short distance into the cave he saw in a remote corner a pair of gray-black, frowzy little cubs, as fat and round as a roll of butter. They were lying upon a soft bed of leaves and grass, which had been collected by their father and mother.

Balser's delight knew no bounds, for, next to his gun, what he wanted above all things was a bear cub, and here were two of them.

Quickly he and his father each picked up a cub and made their way out of the cave.

The cubs, not more than one-half larger than a cat, were round and very fat, and wore a coat of fur, soft and sleek as the finest silk.   Young bears usually are gray until after they are a year old, but these were an exception to the rule, for they were almost black.

Leaving the old bears dead upon the ground, Balser and his father hurried down to the creek, where Mr. Brent washed and dressed his son's wounded arm.   They then marked several trees upon the bank of the creek by breaking twigs, so that they might be able to find the bears when they returned that evening with the horses to take home the meat and skins.

All this, which has taken so long to tell, occurred within the space of a few minutes; but the work while it lasted was hard and tiresome, and, although it was but a short time past noon, Balser and his father were only too glad to turn their faces homeward.

each with a saucy little bear cub under his arm.

" As we have killed their mother," said Balser, referring to the cubs, "we must take care of her children and give them plenty of milk, and bring them up to be good, honest bears."

The evening of the same day Mr. Brent and a few of his neighbours brought home the bear meat and skins.   Balser did not go with his father because his arm was too sore. He was, however, very proud of his wound, and thought that the glory of the day and the two bear cubs were purchased cheaply enough after all.

CHAPTER III.

LOST IN THE FOREST.

BALSER's arm mended slowly, for it had been terribly bitten by the bear. The heavy sleeve of his buckskin jacket had saved him from a wound which might have crippled him for life; but the hurt was bad enough as it was, and Balser passed through many days and nights of pain before it was healed. He bore the suffering like a little man, however, and felt very "big" as he walked about with his arm in a buckskin sling.

Balser was impatient that he could not hunt; but he spent his time more or less satisfactorily in cleaning and polishing his gun and playing with the bear cubs, which his little brother Jim had named "Tom" and "Jerry." The cubs soon became wonderfully tame, and drank eagerly from a pan of milk. They were too small to know how to lap, so the boys put their hands in the pan and held up a finger, at which the cubs sucked lustily. It was very laughable to see the little round black fellows nosing in the milk for the finger. And sometimes they would bite, too, until the boys would snatch away their hands and soundly box the cubs on the ears. A large panful of milk would disappear before you could say "Christmas," and the bears' silky sides would stand out as big and round as a pippin. The boys were always playing pranks upon the cubs, and the cubs soon learned to retaliate. They would climb everywhere about the premises, up the trees, on the roofs of the barn and house, and over the fence. Their great delight was the milk-house and kitchen, where they had their noses into everything, and made life miserable for Mrs. Brent. She would run after them with her broomstick if they but showed their sharp little snouts in the doorway.

Then off they would scamper, yelping as though they were nearly killed, and ponder upon new mischief. They made themselves perfectly at home, and would play with each other like a pair of frisky kittens, rolling over and over on the sod, pretending to fight, and whining and growling as if they were angry in real earnest. One day Balser and his little brother Jim were sitting on a log, which answered the purpose of a settee, under the eaves in front of the house. The boys were wondering what had become of Tom and Jerry, as they had not seen them for an hour or more, and their quietness looked suspicious.

"I wonder if those cubs have run away," said Balser.

"No," said Jim, " bet they won't run away; they've got things too comfortable here to run away. Like as not they're off some place plannin' to get even with us because we ducked them in the water trough awhile ago. They looked awful sheepish when they got out, and as they went off together I jus thought to myself they were goin' away to think up some trick on us."

Balser and Jim were each busily engaged eating the half of a blackberry pie. The eave of the house was not very high, perhaps seven or eight feet from the ground, and Balser and Jim were sitting under it, holding the baby and eating their pie.

Hardly had Jim spoken when the boys heard a scraping sound from above, then a couple of sharp little yelps; and down came Tom and Jerry from the roof, striking the boys squarely on the head.

To say that the boys were frightened does not half tell it. They did not know what had happened. They fell over, and the baby dropped to the ground with a cry that brought her mother to the scene of action in a moment. The blackberry pie had in some way managed to spread itself all over the baby's face, and she was a very comical sight when her mother picked her up.

The bears *had* retaliated upon the boys

sooner than even Jim had anticipated, and
they all had a great laugh over it; the
bears seeming to enjoy it more than anybody else. The boys were ready to admit
that the joke was on them, so they took
the cubs back to the milk-house, and gave
them a pan of rich milk as a peace-offer-
ing.

The scrapes these cubs got themselves
and the boys into would fill a large vol-
ume; but I cannot tell you any more
about them now, as I want to relate an
adventure having no fun in it, which befell
Balser and some of his friends soon after
his arm was well.

It was blackberry time, and several children had come to Balser's home for the
purpose of making a raid upon a large
patch of wild blackberries that grew on the
other side of the river, a half-hour's walk
from Mr. Brent's cabin.

Soon after daybreak one morning, the
little party, consisting of Balser and Jim,
Tom Fox and his sister Liney (which is

"short" for Pau-*li*-ne), and three children from the family of Mr. Neigh, paddled across the river in a canoe which Balser and his father had made from a large gum log, and started westward for the blackberry patch.

Tom and Jerry had noticed the preparations for the journey with considerable curiosity, and felt very much hurt that they were not to be taken along. But they were left behind, imprisoned in a pen which the boys had built for them, and their whines and howls of complaint at such base treatment could be heard until the children were well out of sight of the house.

The party hurried along merrily, little thinking that their journey home would be one of sadness; and soon they were in the midst of the blackberries, picking as rapidly as possible, and filling their gourds with the delicious fruit.

They worked hard all the morning, and the deerskin sacks which they had brought with them were nearly full.

Toward noon the children became hun·gry, and without a dissenting voice agreed to eat dinner.

They had taken with them for lunch a loaf of bread and a piece of cold venison, but Balser suggested that he should go into the woods and find a squirrel or two to help out their meal.   In the meantime Tom Fox had started out upon a voyage of discovery, hoping that he, too, might contribute to the larder.

In a few minutes Balser's gun was heard at a distance, and then again and again, and soon he was back in camp with three fat squirrels.

Almost immediately after him came Tom Fox carrying something in his coonskin cap.

"What have you there, Limpy?" cried Liney.

The children called Tom "Limpy" because he always had a sore toe or a stone bruise on his heel.

"You'll never guess," answered Tom.

All the children took a turn at guessing, and then gave it up.

"Turkey eggs," said Tom. "We'll have eggs as well as squirrel for dinner to-day."

"How will you cook them?" asked one of the Neigh children.

"I'll show you," answered Tom.

So now they were guessing how Limpy would cook the eggs, but he would not tell them, and they had to give it up.

The boys then lighted a fire from the flint-lock on the gun, and Balser, having dressed the squirrel, cut twigs as he had done when he and his father dined on Conn's Creek, and soon pieces of tender squirrel were roasting near the flame, giving forth a most tempting odour.

In the meantime Limpy had gone away, and none of the children knew where he was, or what he was doing.

Soon, however, he returned bearing a large flat rock eight or ten inches in diameter, and two or three inches thick. This rock he carefully washed and scrubbed in a spring, until it was perfectly clean. He then took coals from the fire which Balser had kindled, and soon had a great fire of his own, in the midst of which was the stone. After the blaze had died down, he made a bed of hot coals on which, by means of a couple of sticks, he placed the rock, and then dusted away the ashes.

"Now do you know how I'm going to cook the eggs?" he asked.

They, of course, all knew; and the girls greased the rock with the fat of the squirrel, broke the eggs, and allowed them to fall upon the hot stone, where they were soon thoroughly roasted, and the children had a delicious meal. After dinner they sat in the cool shade of the tree under which they dined, and told stories and asked riddles for an hour or two before they again began berrypicking. Then they worked until about six o'clock, and stopped to have another play before returning home.

They played "Ring around a rosey," 'Squat where ye be," " Wolf," " Dirty dog," and then wound up with the only never-grow-old, " Hide-and-seek."

The children hid behind logs and trees, and in dense clumps of bushes. The boys would often climb trees, when, if "caught," the one who was "it" was sure to run "home" before the hider could slide half-way down his tree. Now and then a hollow tree was found, and that, of course, was the best hiding-place of all.

Beautiful little Liney Fox found one hollow tree too many; and as long as they lived all the children of the party remembered it and the terrible events that followed her discovery. She was seeking a place to hide, and had hurried across a small open space to conceal herself behind a huge sycamore tree. When she reached the tree and went around it to hide upon the opposite side, she found it was hollow at the root

Balser was "it," and with his eyes "hid' was counting one hundred as rapidly and loudly as he could. He had got to sixty, he afterward said, when a shriek reached his ears. This was when Liney found the hollow tree. Balser at once knew that it was Liney's voice; for, although he was but a little fellow, he was quite old enough to have admired Liney's exquisite beauty, and to have observed that she was as kind and gentle and good as she was pretty.

So what wonder that Balser, whom she openly claimed as her best friend, should share not only in the general praise, but should have a boy's admiration for her all his own?

In persons accustomed to exercise the alertness which is necessary for a good hunter, the sense of locating the direction and position from which a sound proceeds becomes highly developed, and as Balser had been hunting almost ever since he was large enough to walk, he knew instantly where Liney was.

He hurriedly pushed his way through the bushes, and in a moment reached the open space of ground, perhaps one hundred yards across, on the opposite side of which stood the tree that Liney had found. Some twenty or thirty yards beyond the tree stood Liney. She was so frightened that she could not move, and apparently had become powerless to scream.

Balser hastened toward her at his utmost speed, and when he reached a point from which he could see the hollow side of the tree, imagine his horror and fright upon beholding an enormous bear emerging from the opening. The bear started slowly toward the girl, who seemed unable to move.

" Run, Liney ! run for your life ! " screamed Balser, who fearlessly rushed toward the bear to attract its attention from the girl, and if possible to bring it in pursuit of himself.

" I just felt," said Balser afterward, " that I wanted to lie down and let the bear eat me at once if I could only keep it away from Liney. I shouted and threw clods and sticks at it, but on it went toward her. I reckon it thought she was the nicest and preferred her to me. It was right, too, for

she was a heap the nicest, and I didn't blame
the bear for wanting her.

"Again I shouted, 'Run, Liney! run!'
My voice seemed to waken her, and she
started to run as fast as she could go, with
the bear after her, and I after the bear as fast
as I could go. I was shouting and doing my
best to make the bear run after me instead
of Liney; but it kept right on after her, and
she kept on running faster and faster into the
dark woods.   In a short time I caught up
with the bear, and kicked it on the side as
hard as I could kick. That made it mad,
and it turned upon me with a furious growl,
as much as to say that it would settle with
me pretty quick and then get Liney.   After
I had kicked it I started to run toward my
gun, which was over by the blackberry
patch. For a while I could hear the bear
growling and puffing right at my heels, and
it made me just fly, you may be sure. I
never ran so fast in all my life, for I knew
that I could not hold out long against the
bear, and that if I didn't get my gun quick

he would surely get me.   I did not care as much as you might think, nor was I very badly frightened, for I was so glad I had saved Liney.   But naturally I wanted to save myself too, if possible, so, as I have said, I ran as I never ran before — or since, for that matter.

"Soon the growls of the bear began to grow indistinct, and presently they ceased and I thought I had left it behind.   So I kept on running toward my gun, and never stopped to look back until I heard another scream from Liney.   Then I looked behind me, and saw that the bear had turned and was again after her, although she was quite a distance ahead of it.

"I thought at first that I should turn back and kick the bear again, and just lie down and let it eat me if nothing else would satisfy it; but I was so near my gun that I concluded to get it and then hurry back and shoot the bear instead of kicking it.

"I heard Liney scream again and heard her call 'B-a-l-s-e-r,' and that made me run even faster than the bear had made me go. It was but a few seconds until I had my gun and had started back to help Liney.

" Soon I was at the hollow sycamore, but the bushes into which Liney had run were so thick and dark that I could see neither her nor the bear. I quickly ran into the woods where I thought Liney had gone, and when I was a little way into the thicket I called to her, but she did not answer. I then went on, following the track of the bear as well as I could. Bears, you know, have long flat feet that do not sink into the ground and leave a distinct track like a deer's foot does, so I soon lost the bear tracks and did not know which way to go.

" I kept going, however, calling loudly for Liney every now and then, and soon I was so deep into the forest that it seemed almost night. I could not see far in any direction on account of the thick underbrush, and at a little distance objects appeared indistinct. On I went, knowing not where, calling 'Liney! Liney!' at nearly every step; but I heard no answer, and it seemed that I liked Liney Fox better than anybody in all the world, and would have given my life to save her."

After Balser had gone into the woods to help Liney the other children gathered in a frightened group about the tree under which they had eaten dinner. There they waited in the greatest anxiety and fear until the sun had almost sunk below the horizon, but Balser and Liney did not return. Shortly before dark the children started homeward, very heavy-hearted and sorrowful, you may be sure. When they reached the river they paddled across and told Mr. Brent that Balser and Liney were lost in the woods, and that when last seen a huge bear was in pursuit of Liney. Balser's father lost not a moment, but ran to a hill near the house, upon the top of which stood a large stack of dry grass, leaves, and wood, placed there for the purpose of signalling the neighbours in case of distress. He at

once put fire to the dry grass, and soon
there was a blaze, the light from which
could be seen for miles around.

Mr. Brent immediately crossed the river,
and leaving Tom Fox behind to guide the
neighbours, walked rapidly in the direction of
the place where Balser and Liney had last
been seen. He took with him the dogs, and
a number of torches which he intended to
light from a tinder-box if he should need
them.

The neighbours soon hurried to the Brent
home in response to the fire signal, and
several of them started out to rescue the
children, if possible. If help were to be
given, it must be done at once. A night in
the woods meant almost certain death to the
boy and girl; for, besides bears and wolves,
there had been for several weeks a strolling
band of Indians in the neighbourhood.

Although the Indians were not brave
enough to attack a settlement, they would
be only too ready to steal the children, did
they but have the opportunity.

These Indians slept all day in dark, secluded spots, and roamed about at night, visiting the houses of the settlers under cover of darkness, for the purpose of carrying off anything of value upon which they could lay their hands.   Recently several houses had been burned, and some twenty miles up the river a woman had been found murdered near the bank.   Two children were missing from another house, and a man while out hunting had been shot by an unseen enemy.

These outrages were all justly attributed to the Indians; and if they should meet Balser and Liney in the lonely forest, Heaven itself only knew what might become of the children, — a bear would be a more merciful enemy.

All night Mr. Brent and the neighbours searched the forest far and near.

Afterward Balser told the story of that terrible night, and I will let him speak : —

" I think it was after six o'clock when I went into the woods in pursuit of Liney and the bear.   It was almost dark at that time in the forest, and a little later, when the sun had gone down and a fine drizzle of rain had begun to fall, the forest was so black that once I ran against a small tree because I did not see it.

"I wandered about for what seemed a very long time, calling for Liney; then I grew hopeless and began to realize that I was lost. I could not tell from which direction I had come, nor where I was going. Everything looked alike all about me—a deep, black bank of nothing, and a nameless fear stole over me. I had my gun, but of what use was it, when I could not see my hand before me? Now and then I heard wolves howling, and it seemed that their voices came from every direction. Once a black shadow ran by me with a snarl and a snap, and I expected every moment to have the hungry pack upon me, and to be torn into pieces. What if they should attack Liney? The thought almost drove me wild.

" I do not know how long I had wandered through the forest, but it must have been eight or nine hours, when I came to the river. I went to the water's edge and put my hand in the stream to learn which way the current ran, for I was so confused and so entirely lost that I did not know which direction was down-stream. I found that the water was running toward my right, and then I climbed back to the bank and stood in helpless confusion for a few minutes.

"Nothing could be gained by standing there watching the water, like a fish-hawk, so I walked slowly down the river. I had been going down-stream for perhaps twenty minutes, when I saw a tall man come out of the woods, a few yards ahead of me, and walk rapidly toward the river bank. He carried something on his shoulder, as a man would carry a sack of wheat, and when he had reached the river bank, where there was more light, I could see from his dress that he was an Indian. I could not tell what it was he carried, but in a moment I thought of Liney and ran toward him. I reached the place where he had gone down the bank just in time to see him place his burden in a canoe. He himself was on the point of stepping in when I called to him to stop, and told him I would shoot him if he did not. My fright was gone in an instant, and I would not have feared all the lions, bears, and Indians that roamed the wilderness. I had but one thought — to save Liney, and something told me that she lay at the other end of the canoe.

" The open space of the river made it light enough for me to see the Indian, and I was so close to him that even in the darkness I could not miss my aim. In place of answering my call, he glanced hurriedly at me, in surprise, and quickly lifted his gun to shoot me. But I was quicker than he, and I fired first. The Indian dropped his gun and plunged into the river. I did not know whether he had jumped or fallen in, but he immediately sank. I thought I saw his head a moment afterward above the surface of the water near the opposite bank, and I do not know to this day whether or not I killed him. At the time 1 did not care, for the one thing on my mind was to rescue Liney.

"I did not take long to climb into the canoe, and sure enough there she was at the other end. I had not taken the precaution to tie the boat to the bank, and I was so overjoyed at finding Liney, and was so eager in my effort to lift her, and to learn if she were dead or alive, that I upset the unsteady thing. I thought we should both drown before we could get out, for Liney was as helpless as if she were dead, which I thought was really the case.

"After a hard struggle I reached shallow water and carried Liney to the top of the bank. I laid her on the ground, and took away the piece of wood which the Indian had tied between her teeth to keep her from crying out. Then I rubbed her hands and face and rolled her over and over until she came to. After a while she raised her head and opened her eyes, and looked about her as if she were in a dream.

"'Oh, Balser!' she cried, and then fainted

away again. I thought she was dead this time sure, and was in such agony that I could not even feel. Hardly knowing what I was doing, I picked her up to carry her home, dead — as I supposed. I had carried her for perhaps half an hour, when, becoming very tired, I stopped to rest. Then Liney wakened up again, and I put her down. But she could not stand, and, of course, could not walk.

"She told me that after she had run into the woods away from the bear, she became frightened and was soon lost. She had wandered aimlessly about for a long time, how long she did not know, but it seemed ages. She had been so terrified by the wolves and by the darkness, that she was almost unconscious, and hardly knew what she was doing. She said that every now and then she had called my name, for she knew that I would try to follow her. Her calling for me had evidently attracted the Indian, whom she had met after she had been in the woods a very long time.

" The Indian seized her, and placed the piece of wood between her teeth to keep her from screaming. He then threw her over his shoulder, and she remembered very little of what happened after that until she was awakened in the canoe by the flash and the report of my gun. She said that she knew at once I had come, and then she knew nothing more until she awakened on the bank. She did not know of the upsetting of the canoe, nor of my struggle in the water, but when I told her about it, she said : —

"' Balser, you've saved my life three times in one night.'

" Then I told her that I would carry her home. She did not want me too, though, and tried to walk, but could not; so I picked her up and started homeward.

"Just then I happened to look toward the river and saw the Indian's canoe floating down-stream, bottom upward. I saw at once that here was an opportunity for us to ride home, so I put Liney down, took off my wet jacket and moccasins, and swam out to

the canoe. After I had drawn it to the bank
and had turned out the water, I laid Liney
at the bow, found a pole with which to guide
the canoe, climbed in myself, and pushed off.
We floated very slowly, but, slow as it was,
it was a great deal better than having to
walk.

"It was just beginning to be daylight when
I heard the barking of dogs. I would
have known their voices among ten thousand, for they were as familiar to me
as the voice of my mother. It was dear
old Tige and Prince, and never in my life
was any voice more welcome to my ears
than that sweet sound. I whistled shrilly
between my fingers, and soon the faithful
animals came rushing out of the woods and
plunged into the water, swimming about us
as if they knew as well as a man could have
known what they and their master had been
looking for all night." Balser's father had
followed closely upon the dogs, and within
an hour the children were home amid the
wildest rejoicing you ever heard.

When Liney became stronger she told how she had seen the hollow in the sycamore tree, and had hurried toward it to hide; and how, just as she was about to enter the hollow tree, a huge bear raised upon its haunches and thrust its nose almost in her face. She said that the bear had followed her for a short distance, and then for some reason had given up the chase. Her recollection of everything that had happened was confused and indistinct, but one little fact she remembered with a clearness that was very curious: the bear, she said, had but one ear.

When Balser heard this, he arose to his feet, and gave notice to all persons present that there would soon be a bear funeral, and that a one-eared bear would be at the head of the procession. He would have the other ear of that bear if he had to roam the forest until he was an old man to find it.

How he got it, and how it got him, I will tell you in the next chapter.

CHAPTER IV.

THE ONE-EARED BEAR.

"You, Tom! You, Jerry! come here!" called Balser one morning, while he and Jim were sitting in the shade near the river in front of the house, overseeing the baby.

"You, Tom! You, Jerry!" called Balser a second time with emphasis. The cubs, snoozing in the sun a couple of paces away, rolled lazily over two or three times in an effort to get upon their feet, and then trotted to their masters with a comical, waddling gait that always set the boys laughing,— it was such a swagger.

When they had come, Balser said, "Stop right there!" and the cubs, being always tired, gladly enough sat upon their haunches, and blinked sleepily into Balser's face, with a greedy expression upon their own, as if to say, "Well, where's the milk?"

"Milk, is it?" asked Balser. "You're always hungry. You're nothing but a pair of gluttons. Eat, eat, from morning until night. Well, this time you'll get nothing. There's no milk for you."

The cubs looked disgusted, so Jim said, and no doubt he was right, for Jim and the cubs were great friends and understood each other thoroughly.

"Now, I've been a good father to you," said Balser. "I've always given you as much milk as you could hold, without bursting, and have tried to bring you up to be good respectable bears, and to do my duty by you. I have whipped you whenever you needed it, although it often hurt me worse than it did you."

The bears grunted, as if to say: "But not in the same place."

"Now what I want," continued Balser, regardless of the interruption, "is, that you tell me what you know, if anything, concerning a big one-eared bear that lives hereabouts. Have you ever heard of him?"

Tom gave a grunt, and Jim, who had been studying bear language, said he meant "Yes."

Jerry then put his nose to Tom's ear, and whined something in a low voice.

"What does he say, Jim?" asked Balser.

"He says for Tom not to tell you anything until you promise to give them milk," answered Jim, seriously.

"Jerry, you're the greatest glutton alive, I do believe," said Balser; "but if you'll tell me anything worth knowing about the one-eared bear, I'll give you the biggest pan of milk you ever saw."

Jerry in his glee took two or three fancy steps, awkwardly fell over himself a couple of times, got up, and grunted to Tom to go ahead. Jim was the interpreter, and Tom grunted and whined away, in a mighty effort to earn the milk.

"The one-eared bear," said he, "is my uncle. Used to hear dad and mother talk about him. Dad bit his ear off. That's how he came to have only one. Dad and he fought about mother, and when dad bit uncle's ear off mother went with dad and wouldn't have anything to do with the other fellow. Couldn't abide a one-eared husband, she said."

"That's interesting," answered Balser. "Where does he live?"

Tom pointed his nose toward the northwest, and opened his mouth very wide.

"Up that way in a cave," interpreted Jim, pointing as the cub had indicated.

"How far is it?" asked Balser.

Jerry lay down and rolled over twice.

"Two hours' walk," said Jim.

"How shall I find the place?" asked Balser.

Tom stood upon his hind legs, and scratched the bark of a tree with his fore paws as high as he could reach.

"Of course," said Balser, "by the bear scratches on the trees. I understand."

Jerry grunted "milk," so Jim said, and

the whole party, boys, bears, and baby, moved off to the milk-house, where the cubs had a great feast.

After the milk had disappeared, Jerry grew talkative, and grunted away like the satisfied little pig that he was.

Again Jim, with a serious face, acted as interpreter.

"Mighty bad bear," said Jerry. "Soured on the world since mother threw him over. Won't have anything to do with anybody. He's as big and strong as a horse, fierce as a lion, and meaner than an Injun. He's bewitched, too, with an evil spirit, and nobody can ever kill him."

"That's the name he has among white folks," remarked Balser.

"Better be careful when you hunt him, for he's killed more men and boys than you have fingers and toes," said Tom. Then the cubs, being full of milk and drowsy, stretched themselves out in the sun, and no amount of persuasion could induce them to utter another grunt.

The bears had told the truth — that is, if they had told anything; for since it had been learned throughout the settlement that it was a one-eared bear which had pursued Liney, many stories had been told of hairbreadth escapes and thrilling adventures with that same fierce prowler of the woods.

One hunter said that he had shot at him as many as twenty times, at short range, but for all he knew, had never even wounded him.

The one-eared bear could not be caught by any means whatsoever. He had broken many traps, and had stolen bait so frequently from others, that he was considered altogether too knowing for a natural bear; and it was thought that he was inhabited by an evil spirit which gave him supernatural powers.

He certainly was a very shrewd old fellow, and very strong and fierce ; and even among those of the settlers who were not superstitious enough to believe that he was inhabited by an evil spirit, he was looked upon as a " rogue " bear; that is, a sullen, morose old fellow, who lived by himself, as old bachelors live.   The bachelors, though, being men, should know better and act more wisely.

Notwithstanding all these evil reports concerning the one-eared bear, Balser clung to his resolution to hunt the bear, to kill him if possible, and to give Liney the remaining ear as a keepsake.

Balser's father knew that it was a perilous undertaking, and tried to persuade the boy to hunt some less dangerous game; but he would not listen to any of the warnings, and day by day longed more ardently for the blood of the one-eared bear.

So one morning shortly after the conversation with the cubs, Balser shouldered his gun and set out toward the northwest, accompanied by Limpy Fox and the dogs.

In truth, the expedition had been delayed that Limpy's sore *toe* might *heal.*   That was one of Liney's jokes.

Limpy had no gun, but he fairly bristled with knives and a hatchet, which for several days he had been grinding and whetting until they were almost as sharp as a razor.

The boys roamed through the forest all day long, but found no trace of the one-eared bear, nor of any other, for that matter. So toward evening they turned their faces homeward, where they arrived soon after sunset, very tired and hungry.

Liney had walked over to Balser's house to learn the fate of the one-eared bear, and fully expected to hear that he had been slaughtered, for she looked upon Balser as a second Saint Hubert, who, as you know, is the patron saint of hunters.

One failure, however, did not shake her faith in Balser, nor did it affect his resolution to kill the one-eared bear.

Next day the boys again went hunting, and again failed to find the bear they sought. They then rested for a few days, and tried again, with still another failure.

After several days of fruitless tramping through the forests, their friends began to laugh at them

" If he ever catches sight of Tom," said Liney, " he'll certainly die, for Tom's knives and hatchet would frighten any bear to death.

Balser also made sport of Tom's arma· ment, but Tom, a little " miffed," said : —

" You needn't be so smart; it hasn't been long since you had nothing but a hatchet. You think because you've got a gun you're very big and cute. I'll bet the time will come when you'll be glad enough that I have a hatchet."

Tom was a truer prophet than he thought, for the day soon came when the hatchet proved itself true steel.

The boys had started out before sun-up one morning, and were deep into the forest when daylight was fairly abroad. Tige and Prince were with them, and were trotting lazily along at the boys' heels, for the day was very warm, and there was no breeze in the forest. They had been walking for several hours, and had almost lost hope, when suddenly a deep growl seemed to come from the ground almost at their feet. The boys sprang back in a hurry, for right in their path stood an enormous bear, where a moment before there had been nothing.

"Lordy! it's the one-eared bear," cried Tom, and the hairs on his head fairly stood on end.

My! what a monster of fierceness the bear was. His head, throat, and paws, were covered with blood, evidently from some animal that he had been eating, and his great red mouth, sharp white teeth, and cropped ear gave him a most ferocious and terrifying appearance.

Balser's first impulse, now that he had found the long-sought one-eared bear, I am sorry to say, was to retreat. That was Tom's first impulse also, and, notwithstanding his knives and hatchet, he acted upon it quicker than a circus clown can turn a somersault.

Balser also started to run, but thought better of it, and turned to give battle to the bear, fully determined to act slowly and deliberately, and to make no mistake about his aim.

He knew that a false aim would end his own days, and would add one more victim to the already long list of the one-eared bear.

The dogs barked furiously at the bear, and did not give Balser an opportunity to shoot. The bear and dogs were gradually moving farther away from Balser, and almost before he knew it the three had disappeared in the thicket. Balser was loath to follow until Tom should return, so he called in an undertone : —

"Tom! Limpy!"

Soon Tom cautiously came back, peering fearfully about him, hatchet in hand, ready to do great execution upon the bear — he afterward said.

"You're a pretty hunter, you are. You'd better go home and get an ax. The bear has got away just because I had to wait for you," said Balser, only too glad to have some one to blame for the bear's escape.

The boys still heard the dogs barking, and hurried on after them as rapidly as the tangle of undergrowth would permit. Now and then they caught a glimpse of the bear, only to lose it again as he ran down a ravine or through a dense thicket. The dogs, however, kept in close pursuit, and loudly called to their master to notify him of their whereabouts.

The boys and bears played at this exciting game of hide-and-seek for two or three hours, but Balser had no opportunity for a good shot, and Tom found no chance to use his deadly hatchet.

When the bear showed a disposition to run away rather than to fight, Limpy grew brave, and talked himself into a high state of heroism.

It was an hour past noon and the boys were laboriously climbing a steep ascent in pursuit of the bear and dogs, which they could distinctly see a few yards ahead of them, at the top of a hill. The underbrush had become thinner, although the shadow of the trees was deep and dark, and Balser thought that at last the bear was his. He repeated over and over to himself his father's

advice: "When you attack a bear, be slow
and deliberate.   Do nothing in a hurry.
Don't shoot until you're sure of your aim."

He remembered vividly his hasty shot
when he wounded the bear on Conn's Creek,
and his narrow escape from death at that
time had so impressed upon him the sound-
ness of his father's advice, that he repeated it
night and morning with his prayers.

When he saw the bear at the top of the
hill, so close to him, he raised his gun to his
shoulder and held it there for a moment,
awaiting a chance for a sure shot.   But dis-
appointment, instead of the bear, was his, for
while he held his gun ready to fire, the bear
suddenly disappeared, as if the earth had
opened and swallowed him.

It all happened so quickly that even the
dogs looked astonished.   Surely, this *was* a
demon bear.

The boys hurried to the spot where they
had last seen the animal, and, although they
carefully searched for the mouth of a cave,
or burrow, through which the bear might

have escaped, they saw none, but found the earth everywhere solid and firm. They extended their search for a hundred feet or more about them, but still with the same result. They could find no hole or opening into which the bear could possibly have entered. His mysterious disappearance right before their eyes seemed terribly uncanny.

There was certainly something wrong with the one-eared bear. He had sprung from the ground, just at their feet, where a moment before there had been nothing; and now he had as mysteriously disappeared into the solid earth, and had left no trace behind him.

Balser and Tom stood for a moment in the greatest amazement, and all they had heard about the evil spirit which inhabited the one-eared bear quickly flashed through their minds.

"We'd better let him go, Balser," said Tom, "for we'll never kill him, that's sure. He's been leading us a wild-goose chase all the morning only to get us up here to kill us. I never saw such an awful place for darkness.

The bushes and trees don't seem natural. They all have thorns and great knots on them, and their limbs and twigs look like huge bony arms and fingers reaching out after us. I tell you this ain't a natural place, and that bear is an evil spirit, as sure as you live. Lordy! let's get out of here, for I never was so scared in my life."

Balser was also afraid, but Tom's words had made him wish to appear brave, and he said: —

"Shucks! Limpy; I hope you ain't afraid when you have your hatchet."

"For goodness' sake, don't joke in such a place as this, Balser," said Tom, with chattering teeth. "I'm not afraid of any natural bear when I have my hatchet, but a bewitched bear is too much for me, and I'm not ashamed to own it."

"How do you know he's bewitched?" asked Balser, trying to talk himself out of his own fears.

"Bewitched? Didn't he come right out of the ground just at our very feet, and didn't he sink into the solid earth right here before our eyes? What more do you want, I'd like to know? Just you try to sink into the ground and see if you can. Nobody can, unless he's bewitched."

Balser felt in his heart that Tom told the truth, and, as even the dogs seemed anxious to get away from the dark, mysterious place, they all descended the hill on the side opposite to that by which they had ascended. When they reached the bottom of the hill they unexpectedly found that they were at the river's edge, and after taking a drink they turned their faces toward home. They thought of dinner, but their appetite had been frightened away by the mysterious disappearance of the bear, and they did not care to eat. So they fed the dogs and again started homeward down the river.

After a few minutes' walking they came to a bluff several hundred feet long, and perhaps fifty feet high, which at that time, the water being low, was separated from the river by a narrow strip of rocky, muddy ground.

This strip of ground was overgrown with reeds and willows, and the bluff was covered with vines and bushes which clung in green masses to its steep sides and completely hid the rocks and earth. Tom was in front, Balser came next, and the dogs, dead tired, were trailing along some distance behind. Suddenly Tom threw up his hands and jumped frantically backward, exclaiming in terrified tones:—

" Oh, Lord! the one-eared bear again."

When Tom jumped backward his foot caught in a vine, and he fell violently against Balser, throwing them both to the ground. In falling, Tom dropped his hatchet, which he had snatched from his belt, and Balser dropped his gun, the lock of which struck a stone and caused the charge to explode. Thus the boys were on their backs and weaponless, while the one-eared bear stood almost within arm's length, growling in a voice like distant thunder, and looking so horrid and fierce that he seemed a **very demon** in a bear's skin.

Tom and Balser were so frightened that for a moment they could not move; but the deep growls which terrified them also brought the dogs, who came quickly to the rescue, barking furiously.

The bear sprang upon the boys just as the dogs came up, and Balser received the full force of a great flat horny paw upon his back, and was almost stunned. The long sharp claws of the bear tore through the buckskin jacket as if it were paper, and cut deep gashes in Balser's flesh. The pain seemed to revive him from the benumbing effect of the stroke, and when the bear's attention was attracted by the dogs, Balser crawled out from beneath the monster and arose to his feet, wounded, bloody, and dizzy.

Tom also felt the force of the bear's great paw, and was lying a few feet from Balser, with his head in a tangle of vines and reeds.

Balser, having escaped from under the bear, the brute turned upon Tom, who was lying prostrate in the bushes.

The dogs were still vigorously fighting

the bear, and every second or two a stroke
from the powerful paw brought a sharp
yelp of pain from either Tige or Prince,
and left its mark in deep, red gashes upon
their bodies.   The pain, however, did not
deter the faithful animals from their efforts
to rescue the boys; and while the bear was
making for Tom it was kept busy in defending itself from the dogs.

In an instant the bear reached Tom, who
would have been torn in pieces at once, had
not Balser quickly unsheathed his long hunting knife and rushed into the fight.   He
sprang for the bear and landed on his back,
clinging to him with one arm about his
neck, while with the other he thrust his
sharp hunting knife almost to the hilt into
the brute's side.

This turned the attack from Tom, and
brought it upon Balser, who soon had his
hands full again.

The bear rose upon his hind feet, and
before Balser could take a step in retreat,
caught him in his mighty arms for the

purpose of hugging him to death, which **is** **a** bear's favourite method of doing battle.

The hunting knife was still sticking in the rough black side of the bear, where Balser had thrust it, and blood flowed from the wound in a great stream.

The dogs were biting at the bear's hind legs, but so intent was the infuriated monster upon killing Balser that he paid no attention to them, but permitted them to work their pleasure upon him, while he was having the satisfaction of squeezing the life out of the boy.

In the meantime Tom recovered and rose to his feet. He at once realized that Balser would be a dead boy if something were not done immediately. Luckily, Tom saw his hatchet, lying a few feet away, and snatching it up he attacked the bear, chopping away at his great back as if it were a tree.

At the third or fourth stroke from Tom's hatchet, the bear loosened his grip upon Balser and fell in a great black heap to the ground, growling and clawing in all direc tions as if he were frantic with rage and pain. He bit at the rocks and bushes, gnashed his teeth, and dug into the ground with his claws.

Balser, when released from the bear, fell in a half conscious condition, close to the river's edge. Tom ran to him, and, hardly knowing what he did, dashed water in his face to remove the blood-stains and to wash the wounds. The water soon revived Balser, who rose to his feet; and, Tom helping his friend, the boys started to run, or rather to walk away as fast as their wounds and bruises would permit, while the dogs continued to bark and the bear to growl.

As the boys were retreating, Tom, turned his head to see if the bear was following, but as it was still lying on the ground, growling and biting at the rocks and scratching the earth, he thought perhaps that the danger was over, and that the bear was so badly wounded that he could not rise, or he certainly would have been on his feet fighting Tige and Prince, who gave him not one moment's peace. Balser and Tom paused for an instant, and were soon convinced that the bear was helpless.

"I believe he can't get up," said Balser.

"Of course he can't," answered Tom, pompously. "I cut his old backbone in two with my hatchet. When he was hugging you I chopped away at him hard enough to cut down a hickory sapling."

The boys limped back to the scene of conflict, and found that they were right. The bear could not rise to his feet, but lay in a huge struggling black heap on the ground.

Balser then cautiously went over to where his gun lay, picked it up, and ran back to Tom. He tried to load the gun, but his arms were so bruised and torn that he could not; so he handed it to Tom, who loaded it with a large bullet and a heavy charge of powder.

Balser then called off the dogs, and Tom, as proud as the President of the United States, held the gun within a yard of the bear's head and pulled the trigger. The great brute rolled over on his side, his mighty limbs quivered, he uttered a last despairing growl which was piteous — for it was almost a groan — and his fierce, turbulent spirit fled forever. Balser then drew his hunting knife from the bear's body, cut off the remaining ear, and put it in the pocket of his buckskin coat.

The boys were sorely wounded, and Balser said that the bear had squeezed his "insides" out of place. This proved to be true to a certain extent, for when he got home it was found that two of his ribs were broken.

The young hunters were only too glad to start homeward, for they had seen quite enough of the one-eared bear for one day.

After walking in silence a short distance down the river, Balser said to Tom: —

"I'll never again say anything bad about your hatchet. It saved my life to-day, and was worth all the guns in the world in such a fight as we have just gone through."

Tom laughed, but was kind-hearted enough not to say, "I told you so."

You may imagine the fright the boys gave their parents when they arrived home wounded, limping, and blood-stained; but soon all was told, and Balser and Tom were the heroes of the settlement.

They had killed the most dangerous animal that had ever lived on Blue River, and had conquered where old and experienced hunters had failed.

The huge carcass of the bear was brought home that evening, and when the skin was removed, his backbone was found to have been cut almost through by Tom's hatchet.

When they cut the bear open somebody said he had two galls, and that fact, it was claimed, accounted for his fierceness.

Where the bear had sprung from when the boys first saw him in the forest, or how he had managed to disappear into the ground at the top of the hill was never satisfactorily explained. Some settlers insisted that he had not been inhabited by an evil spirit, else the boys could not have killed him, but others clung to the belief with even greater faith and persistency.

Liney went every day to see Balser, who was confined to his bed for a fortnight.

One day, while she was sitting by him, and no one else was in the room, he asked her to hand him his buckskin jacket; the one he had worn on the day of the bear fight. The jacket was almost in shreds from the frightful claws of the bear, and tears came to the girl's eyes as she placed it on the bed.

Balser put his hand into one of the deep pockets, and, drawing out the bear's ear, handed it to Liney, saying: —

"I cut this off for you because I like you."

The girl took the bear's ear, blushed a deep red, thanked him, and murmured: —

"And I will keep it, ugly as it is, because I — because — I — like you."

CHAPTER V.

THE WOLF HUNT.

I⟧ was a bright day in August. The whispering rustle of the leaves as they turned their white sides to the soft breath of the southwest wind, the buzzing of the ostentatiously busy bees, the lapping of the river as it gurgled happily along on its everlasting travels, the half-drowsy note of a thrush, and the peevish cry of a catbird seemed only to accentuate the Sabbath hush that was upon all nature.

The day was very warm, but the deep shade of the elms in front of the cabin afforded a delightful retreat, almost as cool as a cellar.

Tom and Liney Fox had walked over to visit Balser and Jim; and Sukey Yates, with her two brothers, had dropped in to stay a

moment or two, but finding such good company, had remained for the day.

The children were seated at the top of the slope that descended to the river, and the weather being too warm to play any game more vigorous than "thumbs up," they were occupying the time with drowsy yawns and still more drowsy conversation, the burden of which was borne by Tom.

Balser often said that he didn't mind "talking parties," if he could only keep Tom Fox from telling the story of the time when he went to Cincinnati with his father and saw a live elephant. But that could never be done; and Tom had told it twice upon the afternoon in question, and there is no knowing how often he would have inflicted it upon his small audience, had it not been for an interruption which effectually disposed of "Cincinnati" and the live elephant for that day.

A bustling old hen with her brood of downy chicks was peevishly clucking about now and then lazily scratching the earth,

and calling up her ever-hungry family whenever she was lucky enough to find a delicious worm or racy bug.

The cubs were stretched at full length in
the bright blaze of the sun, snoring away
like a pair of grampuses, their black silky
sides rising and falling with every breath.
They looked so pretty and so innocent that
you would have supposed a thought of mis-

"MISCHIEF! THEY NEVER THOUGHT OF ANYTHING ELSE."

chief could never have entered their heads.
(Mischief! They never thought of anything
else. From morning until night, and from
night until morning, they studied, planned,
and executed deeds of mischief that would
have done credit to the most freckle-faced
boy in the settlement. Will you tell me why

"BALSER TURNED IN TIME TO SEE A GREAT, LANK, GRAY WOLF EMERGE FROM THE WATER, CARRYING A GANDER BY THE NECK."

it is that the boy most plentifully supplied
with freckles and warts is the most fruitful
in schemes of mischief?) A flock of gray
geese and snowy ganders were floating on
the placid surface of the river, opposite the
children, where a projection of the bank had
caused the water to back, making a little
pool of listless eddies.

Suddenly from among the noiseless flock
of geese came a mighty squawking and a
sound of flapping wings, and the flock, half
flying, half swimming, came struggling at
their utmost speed toward home.

"Look, Balser! Look!" said Liney in a
whisper. "A wolf!"

Balser turned in time to see a great, lank,
gray wolf emerge from the water, carrying a
gander by the neck.

The bird could not squawk, but he flapped
his wings violently, thereby retarding somewhat the speed of Mr. Wolf.

Balser hurried to the house for his gun,
and with Tom Fox quickly paddled across
the river in pursuit of the wolf. The boys

entered the forest at the place the wolf had chosen. White feathers from the gander furnished a distinct spoor, and Balser had no difficulty in keeping on the wolf's track. The boys had been walking rapidly for thirty or forty minutes, when they found that the tracks left by the wolf and the scattered

feathers of the gander led toward a thick clump of pawpaw bushes and vines, which grew at the foot of a small rocky hill. Into this thicket the boys cautiously worked their way, and, after careful examination, they found, ingeniously concealed by dense foliage, a small hole or cleft in the rocks at the base of the hill, and they at once knew that the wolf had gone to earth, and that this was his den.

Foxes make for themselves and their families the snuggest, most ingenious home in the ground you can possibly imagine. They seek a place at the base of a hill or bluff, and dig what we would call in our houses a narrow hallway, straight into the hill. They loosen the dirt with their front feet, and throw it back of them; then with their hind feet they keep pushing it farther toward the opening of the hole, until they have cast it all out. When they have removed the loose dirt, they at once scatter it over the ground and carefully cover it with leaves and vines, to avoid attracting unwelcome visitors to their home.

When the hallway is finished, the fox digs upward into the hill, and there he makes his real home. His reason for doing this is to prevent water from flowing through his hall into his living apartment. The latter is often quite a cave in the earth, and furnishes as roomy and cozy a home for

Mr. and Mrs. Fox and their children as you could find in the world. It is cool in summer and warm in winter. It is softly carpeted with leaves, grass, and feathers, and the foxes lie there snugly enough when the winter comes on, with its freezing and snowing and blowing.

When the fox gets hungry he slips out of his cozy home, and briskly trots to some well-known chicken roost; or perhaps he finds a covey of quails huddled under a bunch of straw. In either case he carries home with him a dainty dinner, and after he has feasted, he cares not how the wind blows, nor how the river freezes, nor how the snow falls, for he is housed like a king, and is as warm and comfortable and happy as if he owned the earth and lived in a palace.

Wolves also make their dens in the earth, but they usually hunt for a place where the hallway, at least, is already made for them. They seek a hill with a rocky base, and find a cave partially made, the entrance to which is a small opening between the rocks. With this for a commencement, they dig out the interior and make their home, somewhat upon the plan of the fox.

The old wolf which Balser and Tom had chased to earth had found a fine dinner for his youngsters, and while the boys were watching the hole, no doubt the wolf family was having a glorious feast upon the gander.

The boys, of course, were at their rope's end. The dogs were not with them, and, even had they been, they were too large to enter the hole leading to the wolf's den. So the boys seated themselves upon a rock a short distance from the opening, and after a little time adopted the follow-ing plan of action.

Balser was to lie upon his breast on the hillside, a few yards above the opening of the wolf den, while Tom was to conceal him-self in the dense foliage, close to the mouth of the cave, and they took their posi-tions accordingly. Both were entirely hid-den by vines and bushes, and remained silent as the tomb. They had agreed that they should lie entirely motionless until the shadow of a certain tree should fall across Tom's face, which they thought would occur within an hour. Then Tom, who could mimic the calls and cries of many birds and beasts, was to squawk like a goose, and tempt the wolf from his den so that Balser could shoot him.

It was a harder task than you may imagine to lie on the ground amid the bushes and leaves; for it seemed, at least so Tom said, that all the ants and bugs and worms in the woods had met at that particular place, and at that exact time, for the sole purpose of "drilling" up and down, and over and around, his body, and to bite him at every step. He dared not move to frighten away the torments, nor to scratch. He could not even grumble, which to Tom was the sorest trial of all.

The moment the shadow of the tree fell upon his face Tom squawked like a goose, so naturally, that Balser could hardly believe

"BANG! WENT BALSER'S GUN, AND THE WOLF . . . PAID FOR HIS FEAST WITH HIS LIFE."

it was Tom, and not a real goose. Soon
he uttered another squawk, and almost at
the same instant Mr. Wolf came out of
his hall door, doubtless thinking to himself that that was his lucky day, for he
would have two ganders, one for dinner
and one for supper, and plenty of cold
goose for breakfast and dinner the next
day. But he was mistaken, for it was the
unluckiest day of the poor wolf's life.
Bang! went Balser's gun, and the wolf,
who had simply done his duty as a father,
by providing a dinner for his family, paid
for his feast with his life.

"We'll drag the body a short distance
away from the den," said Balser, "and you
lie down again, and this time whine like a
wolf. Then the old she-wolf will come out
and we'll get her too."

Tom objected.

"I wouldn't lie there another hour and
let them ants and bugs chaw over me as
they did, for all the wolves in the state."

"But just think, Tom," answered Balser,

"when the wagons go to Brookville this fall we can get a shilling apiece for the wolfskins! Think of it! A shilling! One for you and one for me. I'll furnish the powder and shot if you'll squawk and whine. Squawks and whines don't cost anything, but powder and lead does. Now that's a good fellow, just lie down and whine a little. She'll come out pretty quick."

Tom still refused, and Balser still insisted. Soon Balser grew angry and called Tom a fool. Tom answered in kind, and in a moment the boys clinched for a fight. They scuffled and fought awhile, and soon stumbled over the dead wolf and fell to the ground. Balser was lucky enough to fall on top, and proceeded to pound Tom at a great rate.

"Now will you whine?" demanded Balser.

"No," answered Tom.

"Then take that, and that, and that. Now will you whine?"

"No," cried Tom, determined not to yield.

So Balser went at it again, but there was no give up to stubborn Tom, even if he was on the under side.

At last Balser wiped the perspiration from his face, and, sitting astride of his stubborn foe, said : —

"Tom, if you'll whine I'll lend you my gun for a whole day."

"And powder and bullets?" asked Tom.

"Well, I guess not," answered Balser. "I'll lick you twenty times first."

"If you'll lend me your gun and give me ten full loads, I'll whine till I fetch every wolf in the woods, if the bugs do eat me up."

"That's a go," said Balser, glad enough to compromise with a boy who didn't know when he was whipped.

Then they got up, and were as good friends as if no trouble had occurred between them.

Balser at once lay down upon the hillside above the wolf den, and Tom took his place to whine.

The boys understood their job thoroughly, and Tom's whines soon brought out the old she-wolf. She looked cautiously about her for a moment, stole softly over to her dead mate, and dropped by his side with a bullet through her heart.

Tom was about to rise, but Balser said: —

"Whine again; whine again, and the young ones will come out."

Tom whined, and sure enough, out came two scrawny, long-legged wolf whelps.

The boys rushed upon them, and caught them by the back of the neck, to avoid being bitten, for the little teeth of the pups were as sharp as needles and could inflict an ugly wound. Balser handed the whelp he had caught to Tom, and proceeded to cut two forked sticks from a tough bush, which the children called "Indian arrow." These forked branches the boys tied about the necks of the pups, with which to lead them home.

"CAUGHT THEM BY THE BACK OF THE NECK."

Tom then cut a strong limb from a tree with his pocket-knife. This was quite an undertaking, but in time he cut it through, and trimmed off the smaller branches. The boys tied together the legs of the old wolves and swung them over the pole, which they took upon their shoulders, and started home leading the pups. They arrived home an hour or two before sunset, and found that Liney and Sukey had arranged supper under the elms.

The boys scoured their faces and hands with soft soap, for that was the only soap they had, and sat down to supper with cheeks shining, and hair pasted to their heads slick and tight.

"When a fellow gets washed up this way, and has his hair combed so slick, it makes him feel like it was Sunday," said Tom, who was uneasily clean.

"Tom, I wouldn't let people know how seldom I washed my face if I were you," said Liney, with a slight blush. "They'll think you clean up only on Sunday."

Tom, however, did not allow Liney's re-marks to interrupt his supper, but continued to make sad havoc among the good things on the log.

There was white bread made from wheat flour, so snowy and light that it beat cake "all holler!" the boys "allowed." Wheat bread was a luxury to the settler folks in those days, for the mill nearest to the Blue River settlement was over on Whitewater, at Brookville, fifty miles away. Wheat and the skins of wild animals were the only products that the farmers could easily turn into cash, so the small crops were too precious to be used daily, and wheat flour bread was used only for special occasions, such as Christmas, or New Year's, or com-pany dinner.

Usually three or four of the farmers joined in a little caravan, and went in their wagons to Brookville twice a year. They would go in the spring with the hides of animals killed during the winter, that being the hunting season, and the hides then taken being of

"THE BOYS TIED TOGETHER THE LEGS OF THE OLD WOLVES AND SWUNG THEM OVER THE POLE . . . AND STARTED HOME LEADING THE PUPS."

superior quality to those taken at any other time.

Early in the fall they would go again to Brookville, to market their summer crop of wheat.

Mr. Fox and a few neighbours had returned from an early trip to market only a day or two before the children's party at Balser's home, and had brought with them a few packages of a fine new drink called coffee. That is, it was new to the Western settler, at the time of which I write, milk sweetened with "tree sugar" being the usual table drink.

Liney had brought over a small gourd-ful of coffee as a present to Mrs. Brent, and a pot of the brown beverage had been prepared for the supper under the elms.

The Yates children and Tom were frank enough to admit that the coffee was bitter, and not fit to drink; but Liney had made it, and Balser drank it, declaring it was very good indeed. Liney knew he told a story, but she thanked him for it, nevertheless, and said that the Yates children and Tom were so thoroughly "country" and green that she couldn't expect them to like a civilized drink.

This would have made trouble with Tom, but Balser, who saw it coming, said: —

"Now you shut up, Tom Fox." And Balser had so recently whipped Tom that his word bore the weight of authority.

Besides the coffee and the white bread there was a great gourd full of milk with the cream mixed in, just from the spring-house, delicious and cold. There was a cold loin of venison, which had been spitted and roasted over a bed of hot coals in the kitchen fireplace that morning. There was a gourd full of quail eggs, which had been boiled hard and then cooled in the spring-house. There were heaping plates of fried chicken, and rolls of glorious yellow butter just from the churn, rich with the genuine butter taste, that makes one long to eat it by the spoonful; then there was a delicious apple pie, sweet and crusty, floating in cream almost as thick as molasses in winter.

They were backwoods, homely children; but the supper to which they sat down under the elms was fit for a king, and the appetite with which they ate it was too good for any king.

During the supper the bear cubs had been nosing about the log table, begging each one by turns for a bite to eat. They were so troublesome that Jim got a long stick, and whenever they came within reach he gave them a sharp rap upon the head, and soon they waddled away in a pet of indignant disgust.

For quite a while after Jim had driven them off there had been a season of suspicious quietude on the part of the cubs.

Suddenly a chorus of yelps, howls, growls, and whines came from the direction of the wolf pups. The attention of all at the table was, of course, at once attracted by the noise, and those who looked beheld probably the most comical battle ever fought. Tom and Jerry, with their everlasting desire to have their noses into everything that did not concern them, had gone to investi-gate the wolf pups, and in the course of the investigation a fight ensued, whereby the wolves were liberated. The cubs were the stronger, but the wolves were more active, thus the battle was quite even. The bears, being awkward, of course, were in each other's way most of the time, and would fall over themselves and roll upon the ground for a second or two, before they could again get upon their clumsy feet. The consequence was that the wolves soon had the best of the fight, and, being once free from the cubs, scampered off to the woods and were never seen again.

When the wolves had gone the cubs turned round and round, looking for their late antagonists; but, failing to find them, sat down upon their haunches, grinned at each other in a very silly manner, and then began to growl and grumble in the worst bear language any one had ever heard.

Balser scolded the cubs roundly, and told them he had taught them better than to

swear, even in bear talk.   He then switched
them for having liberated the wolves, and
went back to supper.

The switching quieted the bears for a
short time, but soon their spirit of mischief
again asserted itself.

After another period of suspicious silence
on the part of the cubs, Jim put a general
inquiry to the company: —

"What do you s'pose they're up to this
time?"

"Goodness only knows," responded Balser.
" But if I hear another grunt out of them,
I'll take a stick to them that'll hurt, and
off they'll go to their pen for the night."

The settlers frequently caught swarms
of bees in the woods, and Balser's father
had several hives near the house.   These
hives were called "gums," because they
were made from sections of a hollow gum
tree, that being the best wood for the home
of the bees.   These hollow gums were
placed on end upon small slanting platforms,
and were covered with clapboards, which

were held tightly in their places by heavy stones. There was a small hole, perhaps as large as the end of your finger, cut in the wood at the base, through which the bees entered, and upon the inside of the hive they constructed their comb and stored their honey.

I told you once before how bears delight to eat fish and blackberries. They are also very fond of honey. In fact, bears seem to have a general appetite and enjoy everything, from boys to blackberries.

Hardly had Balser spoken his threat when another duet of howls and yelps reached his ears.

"Now what on earth is it?" he asked, and immediately started around the house in the direction whence the howls had come.

"Geminy! I believe they've upset the bee-gum," said Jim.

"Don't you know they have?" asked Balser. By that time the boys were in sight of the bears.

"THESE HIVES WERE CALLED 'GUMS.'"

" Well, I know now they have, if that suits you any better. Golly! Look at them paw and scratch, and rub their eyes when the bees sting. Good enough for you. Give it to 'em, bees!" And Jim threw back his head and almost split his sides with laughter.

Sure enough, the bears had got to nosing about the bee-gums, and in their ever hungry greediness had upset one. This, of course, made the bees very angry, and they attacked the cubs in a buzzing, stinging swarm that set them yelping, growling, and snapping, in a most desperate and comical manner. All their snapping and growling, however, did no good, for the bees continued to buzz and sting without any indication of being merciful. A little of this sort of thing went a long way with the black mischief-makers, and they soon ran to Balser and Jim for help. The bees, of course, followed, and when the boys and girls saw the bees coming toward them they broke helter-skelter in all directions, and ran as fast as they could go. The bears then ran to the river, and plunged in to escape their tormentors.

When the gum had been placed in position again and the bees had become quiet, the cubs, thinking the field clear, came out of the water dripping wet. Then they waddled up close to the girls, and out of pure mischief shook themselves and sprinkled the dainty clean frocks with a shower from their frowzy hides.

That sealed the fate of the cubs for the day, and when Balser marched them off to their pen they looked so meek and innocent that one would have thought that they had been attending bear Sunday-school all their lives, and were entirely lacking in all unwarrantable and facetious instincts.

They went to bed supperless that evening, but had their revenge, for their yelps and whines kept the whole family awake most of the night.

By the time the bears had been put to bed, darkness was near at hand, so the supper dishes and gourds were washed and carried to the kitchen. Then the visitors said good night and left for home.

CHAPTER VI.

BORROWED FIRE.

ONE day Tom Fox was told by his mother to kindle the fire, which had been allowed to grow so dim that only a smouldering bed of embers was left upon the hearth. Hanging from the crane was a large kettle, almost full of water. Now, in addition to his reputation for freckles, Tom was also believed to be the awkwardest boy in the Blue River settlement. Upon the day above referred to, he did all in his power to live up to his reputation, by upsetting the kettle of water upon the fire, thereby extinguishing the last spark of that necessary element in the Fox household.

Of course there was not a lucifer match on all Blue River, from its source to its mouth; and as Mr. Fox had taken the tinder·

box with him on a hunting expedition, and would not return till night, Limpy received a sound thrashing, and was sent to the house loft, there to ponder for the rest of the day over his misdeeds.

Mrs. Fox then sent Liney over to Mrs. Brent's to borrow fire. Limpy would have been glad to go, had his mother seen fit to send him, but the task would have been a reward rather than a punishment. Liney was delighted to have an opportunity to visit the Brent cabin, so away she went, very willingly indeed. Before the day was finished she was doubly glad she had gone, and the help she was able to give to a friend in need made her devoutly thankful to the kind fate which, operating through Mrs. Fox, had sent her on her errand. The terrible adventure, which befell her, and the frightful — but I am telling my story before I come to it.

When Balser was a boy, each season brought its separate work and recreation on the farm, as it does now. But especially was this true in the time of the early settlers.

The winter was the hunting season. The occupation of hunting, which was looked upon as sport and recreation combined, was also a business with the men who cleared the land and felled the forests of Indiana; for a wagon-load of good pelts, taken during the winter season when the fur is at its best, was no inconsiderable matter, and brought at market more money than the same wagon filled with wheat would have been worth. So the settler of Balser's time worked quite as hard in the winter with his rifle, as he did with his hoe and plough in the fields during the months of summer.

Spring, of course, was the time for breaking up and ploughing. Summer was the wheat harvest. Then, also, the various kinds of wild berries were gathered, and dried or preserved. In the summer casks of rich blackberry wine were made, to warm the cold hunter upon his return from the chase during the cold days to come, or to regale company upon long winter evenings before the blazing fire. Blackberries could

be had by the bushel for the mere gather
ing, and the wine could be made so cheaply
that almost every house was well stocked
with the delicious beverage.

Then came the corn gathering, and bringing in the fodder. The latter was brought
in by wagon-loads, and was stacked against
the sides of the barn and of the cow shed.
It answered a double purpose: it made the
barn and sheds warm and cozy homes for
the stock during the cold bleak winter, and
furnished food for the cattle and the horses,
so that by spring they had eaten part of their
houses. The wheat straw was stacked in the
barnyard; and into this the sheep and calves
burrowed little caves, wherein they would
lie so snug and warm that it made no dif-
ference to them how much the wind blew,
or the snow and rain fell, or how hard it
froze outside; for the bad weather made their
cozy shelter seem all the more comfortable
by contrast.

The fall also had its duties, part task, and
part play. The woods abounded in hickory

nuts, walnuts, and hazelnuts, and a supply of all these had to be gathered, for they furnished no small part of the winter food. Preparation was always made for this work by the boys of Mr. Brent's family long before a hickory nut had thought of falling. Shortly after the wolf hunt which I described to you in the last chapter, Balser and Jim began to make ready for the nut campaign. Their first task was to build a small wagon, for the purpose of carrying home the nuts. They found a tree twelve or fourteen inches in diameter, which they felled. They then sawed off four round sections of the tree, each about one inch thick, to serve as wheels. From the outer edge of these wheels they removed the bark, and bound them with tires made from the iron hoops of a barrel. They then cut round holes in the centre in which to insert the axles of the wagon. With their hatchets they split clapboards, which they made smooth, and of the clapboards they made the bottom, sides, and ends. The boys worked pretty hard for ten or twelve days, and completed as perfect a two-horse wagon, in miniature, as any one ever beheld. There were the tongue, the axletree, the sideboard, the headboard, and the tail-gate and floor, all fitted so tightly together that you would have declared a wagon maker had made them. The wheels, bound with barrel-hoop tires, were marvels of their kind. The wagon bed would hold as much as could be contained in two large flour sacks, and when filled with nuts would prove quite a load to draw, consequently the boys must have a team of some sort. The team which they eventually rigged up was probably the most absurd and curious combination that ever drew a load.

The boys selected strong pieces of deer- hide, and made four sets of harness. For what purpose, do you suppose? You never could guess. Two for the dogs, Tige and Prince, and two for the bear cubs, Tom and Jerry, who they proposed should do some- thing to earn their bread and milk, for they were growing to be great awkward, big-footed, long-legged fellows, and were very strong.

So the four sets of harness were finished, and one day the odd team was hitched up for trial. The little wagon was loaded with rocks, and the boys tried to start the team. The dogs seemed willing enough to obey, but the cubs, which were hitched in front, went every way but the right one, and showed a disposition to rebel against the indignity of work.

The bears were then taken from the lead, the dogs were put in their places, and the bears were put next to the wagon. The team was started again, but the cubs lay down flat upon the ground and refused to move. After trying in vain to induce the cubs to do their duty, Balser spoke to Jim, who was standing at the dogs' heads, and Jim started forward, leading the dogs, and Jim and the dogs dragged after them the cubs and the wagon. At almost every step the heavily loaded wagon would roll upon the hind feet of the cubs, and Balser threw thorns upon the ground, which pricked the bears as they were dragged along, until the black sluggards came to the conclusion that it was easier to work than to be dragged over thorns; so they arose to their feet, and followed the dogs, without, however, drawing an ounce of the load.

The boys kept patiently at this sort of training for three weeks; and at the end of that time, between bribes in the way of milk and honey, and beatings with a thick stick, the cubs little by little submitted to their task, and eventually proved to be real little oxen at drawing a load. The dogs, of course, had been broken in easily.

By the time the cubs were ready for work, the hickory nuts, walnuts, and hazelnuts were ready to be gathered; and the boys only waited for a heavy black frost to loosen the nuts from their shells, and a strong wind to shake them from the branches.

During the summer of which I told you in the preceding chapters, Mr. Brent had raised the roof of his house, so as to make a room in the loft for the boys. This room was floored with rough boards, between which large cracks were left, so that heat from the room below might arise and warm the boys' room. The upper room was reached by the most primitive of stairways. It was nothing more than a small log, or thick pole, with notches cut on each side for footholds, or steps. In going up this stairway the boys climbed hand over hand, and foot over foot, as a bear climbs a tree; and to come down without falling was a task of no small proportions to one inexperienced in the art.

One morning Jim awakened, and looked out from under the warm bearskin which served for a blanket, comforter, and sheet. He listened for a moment to the wind, which was blowing a gale, and then awakened Balser.

"Balser! Balser!" said Jim. "Wake up! There's frost enough to freeze a brass monkey, and the wind is blowing hard enough to blow down the trees, to say nothing of the nuts. Let's get up and have an early start."

Balser was willing, and soon the boys had climbed out from under the warm bearskin, and were downstairs preparing to kindle the fires.

The fire-kindling was no hard task; for the backlog which had been put in the fire-place the evening before was a great roll of red coals, and all that the boys had to do to kindle the fire was to "poke" the backlog, and it fell in chunks of half-charred, burn-ing hickory, that hissed and popped and flamed, and made the room warm before you could say "Jack Robinson." Then the boys threw on a large armful of cut wood, and soon the blaze was crackling cozily, and the kettle singing merrily on the flames.

The morning was cold, and the boys sat upon the great hearth, with their palms to the fire, getting "good and warm for the day," while the gray, frosty dawn was slowly fright-ening the shadows of night away from the forest, to which they seemed to cling.

Then came the mother, who made the breakfast of sweet fried venison, buckwheat-

cakes floating in maple syrup and butter, hoe-
cake, and eggs.   Instead of coffee they drank
warm milk, sweetened with maple sugar,
and I can tell you it was a breakfast to
wax fat on.

The sun was hardly above the horizon,
when breakfast was finished, and the dogs
and cubs were fed.   Then they were har-
nessed to the wagon, and boys, bears, dogs,
and wagon, all started on their way to the
woods.   Hickory trees did not grow plentifully in the bottom-lands, so the boys made
for the hills, perhaps a mile away.

Shortly after they had reached the hills,
Jim cried out : —

"Oh, here's a great big shellbark!   I'll bet
the ground's covered with nuts."

Sure enough, the ground was covered with
them, and the boys filled their wagon in a
very short time.   Then they started home.
The trip home was marred by an upset
owing to the perversity of the cubs ; but the
boys righted the wagon, loaded it with nuts
again, and after considerable trouble de-

posited them safely at home, and went back for another load.

The dog-bear team worked admirably, barring a general tendency to run over logs and stones, and two great loads of hickory nuts were safely brought to the house before dinner.

After the boys, bears, and dogs had eaten a hurried meal, they again went forth in quest of nuts; but they took a different course this time, toward the south — that is, in the direction of the house of Mr. Fox — for the purpose of visiting a hazel thicket, which was a mile from home. Soon the hazel patch was reached, and about five o'clock the wagon was full of beautiful, brown little nuts, than which there is none sweeter.

When the wagon was loaded the boys hitched up the team, much to the delight of the latter, for by that time the dogs and cubs had come to think it great sport, and the caravan moved homeward.

Soon after leaving the hazel patch, the boys entered a dark strip of woods and under growth, through which it was very hard work to draw the wagon. So they attached a long piece of tanned deerskin to the tongue of the wagon, and gave the team a helping hand.

There was but one path through this dark strip of forest over which the wagon could be drawn, and it led through a low piece of ground that was wet and marshy. Upon the soft earth of the path Balser soon noticed the long, broad tracks of a bear, and the dogs at once began to bark and plunge in their harness. The tracks appeared to Balser to be an hour old, so he quieted the dogs, but did not release them from the wagon as he should have done. The boys went forward, regardless of the warning bear tracks, and the dogs and bears, drawing the wagon, followed closely at their heels. As they proceeded the bear tracks became fresher, and Balser began to grow somewhat fearful. Jim had become frightened, and had taken a position at the rear of the wagon to give a helping hand by pushing at the load. He said he could push better than he could pull anyway.

After the little party had got well into the darkest part of the forest, the dogs began to show such evident signs of uneasiness that Balser grasped his gun, and held it in readiness, prepared for a fight, should one become necessary.

The ground had been frozen earlier in the day, but it had thawed, and the path was slippery. Balser, who was walking a short distance ahead of the train, as a sort of advance guard, suddenly stopped and held up his hand warningly to Jim; for right ahead of him in the path stood a huge bear, with its head turned backward, looking inquiringly in the direction of the boys. Jim at once stopped the team. The dogs, of course, were dancing with impatience to be released from the harness, and even the dull-witted bears seemed to realize that something was wrong.

"It's running away," said Balser. "It's not safe to shoot at it from behind. I might wound it, and then we should be the ones to run. What shall we do?"

"Let it run," answered Jim, quickly. "I

don't like to run with a bear after me, any·
way. If you're going to shoot, I'll run now
so as to get a good start."

"No, you don't! You stand right where
you are, and take care of the team. If you
move a foot, I'll lick you," answered Balser,
as he moved cautiously ahead in the direction of the retreating bear.

Jim was frozen by fear to the spot upon
which he stood, as Balser walked out of
sight. In a moment he again heard Balser
speak, and then he heard a loud, deep growl.

The dogs barked and plunged; the cubs
whined and gave forth savage little baby-
bear growls, half whines, for they were only
learning to growl. Jim began to weep and
to scream. Balser, who had disappeared
from sight around a curve in the path, cried
out:—

"Let the dogs loose, for goodness' sake,
Jim! It's after me."

The dogs seemed to understand Balser's
cry better than Jim did; for they barked and
plunged more violently than ever in their

harness.   Jim seemed dazed, and could not, or at least did not, unharness the dogs. Then it was that the good dog sense of old Prince showed itself.   Instead of waiting for help from Jim, who he saw had lost his wits, the good dog began to gnaw at the leather harness which held him and Tige to the wagon, and in a short time the dogs were freed from the wagon, though still tied to each other.

Tige caught inspiration from Prince, and the dogs backed away from each other and pulled with all their strength, until the harness slipped over the head of Prince and left the dogs free.   Then Prince plunged rapidly into the thicket to the rescue of his master, followed closely by Tige, dragging the broken harness.

"Help! help!" cried Balser.   "Why don't you send the dogs?"   And his voice seemed to be going farther and farther away.

"Where are you?" cried Jim, in despair. His terror was so strong upon him that he could not move, and could not have helped

Balser, had he been able to go to him. Jim was a little fellow, you must remember.

"Help! help!" cried Balser again, his voice sounding from a still greater distance. "I've wounded it, and it's about to kill me. Help! help!" but the cries came fainter and fainter.

Jim stood his ground and screamed manfully. Soon after Balser had left Jim and the wagon, the bear turned toward its pursuer and presented to Balser its broadside. This gave the boy a good chance for a shot. For the moment, Balser forgot his father's admonition to be deliberate and to act slowly and his forgetfulness almost cost him his life. Balser shot, and wounded the bear in the neck, but did not kill it. Then it turned, and Balser, fearing to run back upon the path lest he should bring the bear upon Jim, started into the thicket, toward the river, with the bear in hot pursuit. Balser gained rapidly upon the bear at first, but he knew that his advantage could not last, for the bear was sure to catch him soon. What should he do? He hastily went over in his mind the possibilities in the case, and soon determined to put forth his utmost speed to gain as much upon the bear as possible, and then to climb the first tree, of the proper size, to which he should come. With this intent he flung his carbine over his back, by a strap attached to the gun for that purpose, and ran for dear life.

Soon the boy reached a small beech tree, the branches of which were ten or twelve feet from the ground. Up this tree he climbed with the agility of a squirrel. He afterward said:—

"I was so badly scared that it seemed as if my hands and feet had claws like a wild-cat."

The bear had followed so closely upon his track, that, just as the boy was about to draw himself up among the branches of the tree, the bear rose upon its hind legs and caught the boy's toes between his teeth. Balser screamed with pain, and tried to draw his foot away; but the harder he pulled the harder pulled the bear, and the pain was so great that he thought he could not stand it. While he clung to the limb with one hand, he reached toward the bear with the other, and caught it by the nose. He twisted the bear's nose until the brute let loose of his foot. Then he quickly drew himself into the tree, and seated himself none too soon astride of a limb.

When Balser had fixed himself firmly on the limb he proceeded at once to load his gun. This was no slight matter under the circumstances; for, aside from the fact that his position in the tree was an uneasy one, the branches were in his way when he began to use his ramrod. Balser had hardly poured the powder into his gun, when the bear again rose on its hind legs, and put its front paws upon the body of the tree, with evident intent to climb after the boy who had wounded it and had so insultingly twisted its nose. Bears like to scratch the bark of trees, and seem to take the same pride in placing their marks high upon the tree trunks that a young man does in making a long jump or a good shot. Vanity, in this case, proved to be the bear's undoing, as it has often been with men and boys. When it was reaching upward to make a high scratch, that it thought would be the envy of every bear that would see it, it should have been climbing; for while it was scratching Balser was loading, Not hurriedly, as he had shot, but slowly and deliberately, counting one, two, three with every movement; for when he had shot so hurriedly a few minutes before and had only wounded the bear, he had again learned the great lesson to make haste slowly. The lesson was to be impressed upon Balser's mind more firmly than ever before he was through with the wounded bear; for to the day of his death he never forgot the events which befell him after he came down from the tree. Although Balser was deliberate, he had no time to waste, for soon the bear began climbing the tree, aided by a few small branches upon the lower part of the trunk, which had given help to Balser. Up the bear went, slowly and surely. Its great red tongue hung out at one side of its mouth, and its black, woolly coat was red and gory with blood from the wound that Balser had inflicted upon its huge neck. Its sharp little eyes were fixed upon Balser, and seemed to blaze with fury and rage, and its long bright teeth gleamed as its lips were drawn back in anger when it growled. Still the bear climbed, and still Balser was loading his gun. Would he have it loaded before the bear reached him? Now the powder was all in — a double charge. Now the first patch was in, and Balser was trying to ram it home. The branches of the trees were in his way, and the ramrod would not go into the gun. Inanimate things are often stubborn just when docility is most needed. Ah! At last the ramrod is in, and the first patch goes home, hard and fast upon the powder. On comes the bear, paw over paw, foot over foot, taking its time with painful deliberation and, bearlike, carefully

choosing its way; for it thinks full sure the
boy cannot escape. Hurriedly Balser reaches
into his pouch for a bullet. He finds one
and puts it to the muzzle of his gun. Ah!
worse luck! The bullet will not go in. It
is too large. Balser feels with his finger a
little ridge extending around the bullet, left
there because he had not held the bullet
moulds tightly together when he had cast
the bullet. The boy impatiently throws the
worthless bullet at the bear and puts his
hand into the pouch for another. This
time the bullet goes in, and the ramrod
drives it home. Still there is the last patch
to drive down, — the one which holds the
bullet, — and still the bear climbs toward
its intended victim. Its growls seem to
shake the tree and its eyes look like burning
embers. The patches and the bullets Balser
kept in the same pouch, so, when the bullet
has been driven home, the boy's hand again
goes into the pouch for the last patch. He
can find nothing but bullets. Down goes
his hand to each corner of the pouch in

search of a patch; but alas! the patch, like
a false friend, is wanting when most needed.
On comes the bear. Not a moment is to be
lost. A patch must be found; so the boy
snatches off his cap of squirrel skin, and
with his teeth bites out a piece of the skin
which will answer his purpose. Then he
dashes the mutilated cap in the bear's face,
only a foot or two below him. Quickly is
the squirrel-skin patch driven home, but
none too quickly, for the bear is at Balser's
feet, reaching for him with his great, rough,
horny paw, as a cat reaches for a mouse.
Balser quickly lifts himself to the limb above
him, and hurriedly turning the muzzle of
his gun right into the great red mouth,
pulls the trigger. Bang! And the bear
falls to the ground, where it lies apparently
dead. It was only apparently dead, though,
as you will presently see. Balser breathed a
sigh of relief as the bear fell backward, for
he was sure that he had killed it. No bear,
thought he, could survive a bullet driven by
the heavy charge of powder behind the one

which had sped so truly into the bear's mouth. Again Balser failed to make haste slowly. He should have remained in his secure position until he was sure that the bear was really dead; for a badly wounded bear, although at the point of death, is more dangerous than one without a scar. Without looking at the bear Balser called Jim to come to him, and began climbing down the tree, with his carbine slung over his shoulder, and his back to the bear. All this happened in a very short space of time. In fact, the time during which Balser was loading his gun, and while the bear was climbing the tree, was the same time in which the dogs were freeing themselves from the wagon; and Balser's second shot was heard by Jim just as the dogs went bounding off to Balser's relief. When the boy jumped to the ground, lo! the bear was alive again, and was on its feet, more ferocious than ever, and more eager for fight. Like our American soldiers, the bear did not know when it was whipped.

At the time the dogs bounded away from Jim, there came down the path toward him a young girl. Who do you think it was? Liney Fox. She was carrying in her hand a lighted torch, and was swinging it gently from side to side that she might keep it ablaze. This was the fire which Liney had been sent to borrow. She had heard Balser's cry and had heard both the shots that Balser had fired. She ran quickly to Jim, and with some difficulty drew from him an explanation of the situation. Then, as the dogs bounded away, she followed them, feeling sure that their instinct would lead them to Balser. The girl's strength seemed to be increased a thousand fold, and she ran after the dogs in the hope that she might help the boy who had saved her life upon the night when she was lost in the forest. How could she help him? She did not know; but she would at least go to him and do her best.

Just as Balser reached the ground, the bear raised itself upon its hind feet and struck at the boy, but missed him. Then Balser ran to the side of the tree opposite the bear, and bear and boy for a few moments played at a desperate game of hide-and-seek around the tree. It seemed a very long time to Balser. He soon learned that the bear could easily beat him at the game, and in desperation he started to run toward the river, perhaps two hundred yards away. He cried for help as he ran, and at that moment the dogs came up, and Liney followed in frantic, eager haste after them. Balser had thrown away his gun, and was leading the bear in the race perhaps six or eight feet. Close upon the heels of the bear were the dogs, and closer than you would think upon the heels of the dogs came Liney. Her bonnet had fallen back and her hair was flying behind her, and the torch was all ablaze by reason of its rapid movement through the air.

At the point upon the river's bank toward which Balser ran was a little stone cliff, almost perpendicular, the top of which was

eight or ten feet from the water. Balser
had made up his mind that if he could reach
this cliff he would jump into the river, and
perhaps save himself in that manner. Just
as the boy reached the edge of the cliff
Liney unfortunately called out "Balser!"

Her voice stopped him for a moment, and
he looked back toward her. In that moment the bear overtook him and felled him
to the ground with a stroke of its paw.
Balser felt benumbed and was almost sense-
less. Instantly the bear was standing over
him, and the boy was blinded by the stream
of blood which flowed into his eyes and
over his face from the wound in the bear's
great mouth. He felt the bear shake him
as a cat shakes a mouse, and then for a
moment the sun seemed to go out, and
all was dark. He could see nothing. He
heard the dogs bark, as they clung to the
bear's ears and neck close to his face, and
he heard Liney scream; but it all seemed
like a far-away dream. Then he felt something burn his face, and sparks and hot

ashes fell upon his skin and blistered him.
He could not see what was happening, but
the pain of the burns seemed to revive him,
and he was conscious that he was relieved
from the terrible weight of the bear upon
his breast. This is what happened: after
Balser had fallen, the dogs had held the
bear's attention for a brief moment or two,
and had given Liney time to reach the scene
of conflict. The bear had caught Balser's
leather coat between its jaws, and was shaking him just as Liney came up. It is
said that the shake which a cat gives a
mouse produces unconsciousness; and so it
is true that the shake which the larger animals give to their prey before killing it has
a benumbing effect, such as Balser felt.
When Liney reached Balser and the bear,
she had no weapon but her torch, but with
true feminine intuition she did, without stopping to think, the only thing she could do,
and for that matter the best thing that any
one could have done. She thrust the burning torch into the bear's face and held it

there, despite its rage and growls. Then it was that Balser felt the heat and sparks, and then it was that the bear, blinded by the fire, left Balser. The bear was frantic with pain, and began to rub its eyes and face with its paws, just as a man would do under the same circumstances. It staggered about in rage and blindness, making the forest echo with its frightful growls, until it was upon the edge of the little precipice of which I have spoken. Then Liney struck it again with her burning torch, and gave it a push, which, although her strength was slight, sent the bear rolling over the cliff into the river. After that she ran back to Balser, who was still lying upon the ground, covered with blood. She thought he was terribly wounded, so she tore off her muslin petticoat, and wiped the blood from Balser's face and hands. Her joy was great when she learned that it was the bear's blood and not Balser's that she saw. The boy soon rose to his feet, dazed and half blinded.

"Where's the bear?" he asked.

"We pushed him into the river," said Jim, who had come in at the last moment.

"Yes, 'we pushed him in,'" said Balser, in derision. "Liney, did you —"

"Yes," answered Liney. "I don't know how I did it; but after I had put my torch in the bear's face, when he was over you, I — I pushed him into the river." And she cast down her sweet, modest eyes, as if ashamed of what she had done.

"Liney, Liney —" began Balser; but his voice was choked by a great lump of sobs in his throat. "Liney, Liney —" he began again; but his gratitude was so great he could not speak. He tried again, and the tears came in a flood.

"Cry-baby!" said Jim.

"Jim, you're a little fool," said Liney, turning upon the youngster with a blaze of anger in her eyes.

"Jim's right," sobbed Balser. "I — I am a c-c-cry-baby."

"No, no! Balser," said Liney, soothingly.

as she took his hand. " I know. I under
stand without you telling me."

" Yes," sobbed Balser, " I — I — c-c-cry —
because — I — thank you so much."

" Don't say that, Balser," answered Liney.
" Think of the night in the forest, and think
of what you did for me."

" Oh! But I'm a boy."

Balser was badly bruised, but was not
wounded, except in the foot where the bear
had caught him as he climbed the tree.
That wound, however, was slight, and would
heal quickly. The cubs had broken away
from the loaded wagon, and Jim, Liney,
Balser, dogs, and cubs all marched back to
Mr. Brent's in a slow and silent procession,
leaving the load of nuts upon the path, and
the bear dead upon a ripple in the river.

CHAPTER VII.

THE FIRE BEAR.

ONE evening in December, a few weeks after Liney had saved Balser's life by means of the borrowed fire, Balser's father and mother and Mr. and Mrs. Fox, went to Marion, a town of two houses and a church, three miles away, to attend "Protracted Meeting." Liney and Tom and the Fox baby remained with Balser and Jim and the Brent baby, at the Brent cabin.

When the children were alone Liney proceeded to put the babies to sleep, and when those small heads of their respective households were dead to the world in slumber, rocked to that happy condition in a cradle made from the half of a round, smooth log, hollowed out with an adze, the other children huddled together in the fireplace to talk and to play games. Chief among the games was that never failing source of delight, "Simon says thumbs up."

Outside the house the wind, blowing through the trees of the forest, rose and sank in piteous wails and moans, by turns, and the snow fell in angry, fitful blasts, and whirled and turned, eddied and drifted, as if it were a thing of life. The weather was bitter cold; but the fire on the great hearth in front of the children seemed to feel that while the grown folks were away it was its duty to be careful of the children, and to be gentle, tender, and comforting to them; so it spluttered, popped, and cracked like the sociable, amiable, and tender-hearted fire that it was. It invited the children to go near it and to take its warmth, and told, as plainly as a fire could, — and a fire can talk, not English perhaps, but a very understandable language of its own, — that it would not burn them for worlds. So, as I said, the children sat inside the huge fireplace, and cared little whether or not the cold north wind blew.

After "Simon" had grown tiresome, Liney told riddles, all of which Tom, who had heard them before, spoiled by giving the answer before the others had a chance to guess. Then Limpy propounded a few riddles, but Liney, who had often heard them, would not disappoint her brother by telling the answers. Balser noticed this, and said, "Limpy, you ought to take a few lessons in good manners from your sister."

"Why ought I?" asked Tom, somewhat indignantly.

"Because she doesn't tell your riddles as you told hers," answered Balser.

"He wants to show off," said Jim.

"No, he doesn't," said Liney. But she cast a grateful glance at Balser, which said, "Thank you" as plainly as if she had spoken the words. Tom hung his head, and said he didn't like riddles anyway.

"Let's crack some nuts," proposed Jim, who was always hungry.

This proposition seemed agreeable to all, so Balser brought in a large gourd filled

with nuts, and soon they were all busy crack
ing and picking.

Then Liney told stories from "The Pilgrim's Progress" and the Bible. She was at
the most thrilling part of the story of Daniel
in the lions' den, and her listeners were
eager, nervous, and somewhat fearful, when
the faint cry of "Help!" seemed to come
right down through the mouth of the
chimney.

"Listen!" whispered Balser, holding up
his hands for silence. In a moment came
again the cry, "Help!" The second cry
was still faint, but louder than the first; and
the children sprang together with a common
impulse, and clung to Balser in unspoken
fear.

"Help! help!" came the cry, still nearer
and louder.

"Some one wants help," whispered Balser.
"I—must—go—to—him." The latter
clause was spoken rather hesitatingly.

"No, no!" cried Liney. "You must not
go. It may be Indians trying to get you

out there to kill you, or it may be a ghost
You'll surely be killed if you go."

Liney's remark somewhat frightened
Balser, and completely frightened the other
children; but it made Balser feel all the
more that he must not be a coward before
her. However much he feared to go in
response to the cry for help, he must not let
Liney see that he was afraid. Besides, the
boy knew that it was his duty to go; and
although with Balser the sense of duty
moved more slowly than the sense of fear,
yet it moved more surely. So he quickly
grasped his gun, and carefully examined the
load and priming. Then he took a torch,
lighted it at the fire, and out he rushed into
the blinding, freezing storm.

"Who's there?" cried Balser, holding his
torch on high.

"Help! help!" came the cry from a short
distance down the river, evidently in the
forest back of the barn. Balser hurried in
the direction whence the cry had come, and
when he had proceeded one hundred yards

or so, he met a man running toward him almost out of breath from fright and exhaustion. Balser's torch had been extinguished by the wind, snow, and sleet, and he could not see the man's face.

"Who are you, and what's the matter with you?" asked brave little Balser, meanwhile keeping his gun ready to shoot, if need be.

"Don't you know me, Balser?" gasped the other.

"Is it you, Polly?" asked Balser. "What on earth's the matter?"

"The Fire Bear! The Fire Bear!" cried Poll. "He's been chasin' me fur Lord knows how long. There he goes! There! Don't you see him? He's movin' down to the river. He's crossin' the river on the ice now. There! There!" And he pointed in the direction he wished Balser to look. Sure enough, crossing on the ice below the barn, was the sharply defined form of a large bear, glowing in the darkness of the night as if it were on fire

This was more than even Balser's courage could withstand; so he started for the house as fast as his legs could carry him, and Polly came panting and screaming at his heels.

Polly's name, I may say, was Samuel Parrott. He was a harmless, simple fellow, a sort of hanger-on of the settlement, and his surname, which few persons remembered, had suggested the nickname of Poll, or Polly, by which he was known far and wide.

By the time Balser had reached the house he was ashamed of his precipitate retreat, and proposed that he and Polly should go out and further investigate the Fire Bear.

This proposition met with such a decided negative from Polly, and such a vehement chorus of protests from Liney and the other children, that Balser, with reluctance in his manner, but gladness in his heart, consented to remain indoors, and to let the Fire Bear take his way unmolested.

"When did you first see him?" asked Balser of Polly Parrot.

"'Bout a mile down the river, by Fox's Bluff," responded Polly. "I've been runnin' every step of the way, jist as hard as I could run, and that there Fire Bear not more'n ten feet behind me, growlin' like thunder, and blazin' and smokin' away like a bonfire."

"Nonsense," said Balser. "He wasn't blazing when I saw him."

"Of course he wasn't," responded Poll. "He'd about burned out. D'ye think a bear could blaze away forever like a volcano?" Poll's logical statement seemed to be convincing to the children.

"And he blazed up, did he?" asked Liney, her bright eyes large with wonder and fear.

"Blazed up!" ejaculated Polly. "Bless your soul, Liney, don't you see how hot I am? Would a man be sweatin' like I am on such a night as this, unless he's been powerful nigh to a mighty hot fire?"

Poll's corroborative evidence was too strong for doubt to contend against, and a depressing conviction fell upon the entire company, including Balser, that it was really the Fire Bear which Polly and Balser had seen. Although Balser, in common with most of the settlers, had laughed at the stories of the Fire Bear which had been told in the settlement, yet now he was convinced, because he had seen it with his own eyes. It was true that the bear was not ablaze when he saw him, but certainly he looked like a great glowing ember, and, with Polly's testimony, Balser was ready to believe all he had heard concerning this most frightful spectre of Blue River, the Fire Bear.

One of the stories concerning the Fire Bear was to the effect that when he was angry he blazed forth into a great flame, and that when he was not angry he was simply aglow. At times, when the forests were burned, or when barns or straw-stacks were destroyed by fire, many persons, especially of the ignorant class, attributed the incendiarism to the Fire Bear. Others, who pretended to more wisdom, charged the Indians with the crimes. Of the latter class had been Balser. But to see is to believe.

Another superstition about the Fire Bear was, that any person who should be so unfortunate as to behold him would die within three months after seeing him, unless perchance he could kill the Fire Bear,—a task which would necessitate the use of a potent charm, for the Fire Bear bore a charmed life. The Fire Bear had been seen, within the memory of the oldest inhabitant, by eight or ten persons, always after night. Each one who had seen the bear had died within the three months following. He had been stalked by many hunters, and although several opportunities to kill him had occurred, yet no one had accomplished that much-desired event.

You may be sure there were no more games, riddles, or nut-cracking that evening in the Brent cabin. The children stood for a few moments in a frightened group, and then took their old places on the logs inside the fireplace. Polly, who was stupid with fright, stood for a short time silently facing the fire, and then said mournfully: "Balser, you and me had better jine the church. We're goners inside the next three months, — goners, just as sure as my name's Polly." Then meditatively, "A durned sight surer than that; for my name ain't Polly at all; but Samuel, or Thomas, or Bill, or something like that, I furgit which; but we're goners, Balser, and we might as well git ready. No livin' bein' ever seed that bear and was alive three months afterwards."

Then Liney, who was sitting next to Balser, touched his arm gently, and said: —

"I saw him too. I followed you a short way when you went out, and I saw something bright crossing the river on the ice just below the barn. Was that the bear?"

"Yes, yes," cried Balser. "For goodness' sake, Liney, why didn't you stay in the house?"

"You bet I stayed in," said Jim.

"And so did I," said Tom.

No one paid any attention to what Jim and Limpy said, and in a moment Liney was weeping gently with her face in her hands.

Jim and Limpy then began to cry, and soon Polly was boohooing as if he were already at the point of death. It required all of Balser's courage and strength to keep back the tears, but in a moment he rose to his feet and said: "Stop your crying, everybody. I'll kill that bear before the three months is half gone; yes, before a month has passed. If Liney saw him, the bear dies; that settles it."

Liney looked up to Balser gratefully, and then, turning to Polly, said:—

"He'll save us, Polly; he killed the one-eared bear, and it was enough sight worse to fight than the Fire Bear. The one-eared bear was a — was a devil."

Polly did not share Liney's confidence; so he sat down upon the hearth, and gazed sadly at the fire awhile. Then, taking his elbow for his pillow, he lay upon the floor and moaned himself to sleep.

The children sat in silence for a short time; and Jim lay down beside Polly, and closed his eyes in slumber. Then Limpy's head began to nod, and soon Limpy was in the land of dreams. Balser and Liney sat upon the spare backlog for perhaps half an hour, without speaking.

The deep bed of live coals cast a rosy glow upon their faces, and the shadows back in the room grew darker, as the flame of the neglected fire died out. Now and then a fitful blaze would start from a broken ember, and the shadows danced for a moment over the floor and ceiling like sombre spectres, but Balser and Liney saw them not.

Despite their disbelief in the existence of the Fire Bear, the overwhelming evidence of the last two hours had brought to them a frightful conviction of the truth of all they had heard about the uncanny, fatal monster. Three short months of life was all that was left to them. Such had been the fate of all

who had beheld the Fire Bear. Such certainly would be their fate unless Balser could
kill him — an event upon which Liney built
much greater hope than did Balser.

After a long time Balser spoke, in a low
tone, that he might not disturb the others: —

"Liney, if I only had a charm, I might
kill the Fire Bear; but a gun by itself can
do nothing against a monster that bears a
charmed life. We must have a charm.
You've read so many books and you know
so much; can't you think of a charm that
would help me?"

"No, no, Balser," sighed Liney, "you know
more than I, a thousand times."

"Nonsense, Liney. Didn't you spell down
everybody — even the grown folks — over at
Caster's bee?"

"Yes, I know I did; but spelling isn't
everything, Balser. It's mighty little, and
don't teach us anything about charms. You
might know how to spell every word in a big
book, and still know nothing about charms."

"I guess you're right," responded Balser,

dolefully. " I wonder how we can learn to make a charm."

" Maybe the Bible would teach us," said Liney. " They say it teaches us nearly everything."

" I expect it would," responded Balser. " Suppose you try it."

" I will," answered Liney. Silence ensued once more, broken only by the moaning wind and the occasional popping of the backlog.

After a few minutes Liney said in a whisper : —

" Balser, I've been thinking, and I'm going to tell you about something I have. It's a great secret. No one knows of it but mother and father and I. I believe it's the very thing we want for a charm. It looks like it, and it has strange words engraved upon it."

Balser was alive with interest.

" Do you promise never to tell any one about it?" asked Liney.

" Yes, yes, indeed. Cross my heart, 'pon honour, hope to die."

Balser's plain, unadorned promise was enough to bind him to secrecy under ordinary circumstances, for he was a truthful boy; but when his lips were sealed by such oaths as " Cross my heart," and " Hope to die," death had no terrors which would have forced him to divulge.

" What is it?   Quick, quick, Liney! "

" You'll never tell? "

" No, cross my — "

" Well, I'll tell you.   I've a thing at home that's almost like a cross, only the pieces cross each other in the middle and are broad at each end.   It's a little larger than a big button.   It's gold on the back and has a lot of pieces of glass, each the size of a small pea, on the front side.   Only I don't believe they're glass at all.   They are too bright for glass.   You can see them in the dark, where there's no light at all.   They shine and glitter and sparkle, so that it almost makes you blink your eyes.   Now you never saw glass like that, did you? "

" No," answered Balser, positively.

Liney continued; "That's what makes me think it's a charm; for you couldn't see it in the dark unless it was a charm, could you, Balser?"

"I should think not."

"There's a great big piece of glass, or whatever it is, in the centre of it — as big as a large pea, and around this big piece are four words in some strange language that nobody can make out,— at least, mother says that nobody in this country can make them out. Mother told me that the charm was given to her for me by a gypsy man, when I was a baby. Mother says there's something more to tell me about it when I become a woman. Maybe that's the charm of it; I'm sure it is." And she looked up to Balser with her soft, bright eyes full of inquiry and hope.

"I do believe that thing is a charm," said Balser. Then meditatively: "I know it's a charm. Don't tell me, Liney, that you don't know a lot of things."

Liney's sad face wore a dim smile of satis-faction at Balser's compliments, and again they both became silent. Balser remained in a brown study for a few moments, and then asked : —

"Where does your mother keep the — the charm?"

"She keeps it in a box under my bed."

"Good! good!" responded Balser. "Now I'll tell you what to do to make it a sure enough charm."

"Yes, yes," eagerly interrupted Liney.

"You take the charm and hold it on your lips while you pray seven times that I may kill the bear. Do that seven times for seven nights, and on the last night I'll get the charm, and Polly, Limpey, and I will go out and kill the bear, just as sure as you're alive."

The plan brought comfort to the boy and girl.

Soon Liney's eyes became heavy, and she fell asleep; and as Balser looked upon her innocent beauty, he felt in his heart that if seven times seven prayers from Liney's lips could not make a charm which would give him strength from on high to kill the bear, there was no strength sufficient for that task to be had any place.

Late in the night — nine o'clock — the parents of the children came home. The sleepers were aroused, and all of them tried to tell the story of the Fire Bear at one and the same time.

"Tell me about it, Balser," said Mr. Fox, seriously; for he, too, was beginning to believe in the story of the Fire Bear. Then Balser told the story, assisted by Polly, and the strange event was discussed until late into the night, without, however, the slightest reference to the charm by either Balser or Liney. That was to remain their secret.

Mr. and Mrs. Fox remained with the Brents all night, and before they left next morning, Liney whispered to Balser: —

"I'll begin to-night, as you told me to do, with the charm. Seven nights from this the charm will be ready — if I can make it."

"And so will I be ready," answered Balser, and both felt that the fate of the Fire Bear was sealed.

CHAPTER VIII.

THE BLACK GULLY.

NOTE. — The author, fearing that the account of fire spring
ing from the earth, given in the following story, may be
considered by the reader too improbable for any book but one
of Arabian fables, wishes to say that the fire and the explosion occurred in the place and manner described.

THE Fire Bear had never before been seen
in the Blue River neighbourhood. His former appearances had been at or near the
mouth of Conn's Creek, where that stream
flows into Flatrock, five or six miles southeast of Balser's home.

Flatrock River takes its name from the
fact that it flows over layers of broad flat
rocks. The soil in its vicinity is underlaid
at a depth of a few feet by a formation of
stratified limestone, which crops out on the
hillsides and precipices, and in many places
forms deep, cañon-like crevasses, through
which the river flows. In these cliffs and

miniature cañons are many caves, and branching off from the river's course are many small side-cañons, or gullies, which at night are black and repellent, and in many instances are quite difficult to explore.

One of these side-cañons was so dark and forbidding that it was called by the settlers "The Black Gully." The conformation of the rocks composing its precipitous sides was grotesque in the extreme; and the overhanging trees, thickly covered with vines, cast so deep a shadow upon the ravine that even at midday its dark recesses bore a cast of gloom like that of night untimely fallen. How Balser happened to visit the Black Gully, and the circumstances under which he saw it—sufficiently terrible and awe-inspiring to cause the bravest man to tremble — I shall soon tell you.

The country in the vicinity of Flatrock was full of hiding-places, and that was supposed to be the home of the Fire Bear.

The morning after Polly and Balser had seen the Fire Bear, they went forth bright and early to follow the tracks of their fiery enemy, and if possible to learn where he had gone after his unwelcome visit.

They took up the spoor at the point where the bear had crossed the river the night before, and easily followed his path three or four miles down the stream. There they found the place where he had crossed the river to the east bank. The tracks, which were plainly visible in the new-fallen snow, there turned southeast toward his reputed home among the caves and gullies of Flat-rock and Conn's Creek.

The trackers hurried forward so eagerly in their pursuit that they felt no fatigue. They found several deer and at one time they saw at a great distance a bear; but they did not pursue either, for their minds were too full of the hope that they might discover the haunts of the monster upon whose death depended, as they believed, their lives and that of Liney Fox. When Balser and Polly reached the stony ground of Flatrock the bear tracks began to grow indistinct, and soon they were lost entirely among the smooth rocks from which the snow had been blown away. The boys had, however, accomplished their purpose, for they were convinced that they had discovered the haunts of the bear. They carefully noticed the surrounding country, and spoke to each other of the peculiar cliffs and trees in the neighbourhood, so that they might remember the place when they should return. Then they found a dry little cave wherein they kindled a fire and roasted a piece of venison which they had taken with them. When their roast was cooked, they ate their dinner of cold hoe-cake and venison, and then sat by the fire for an hour to warm and rest before beginning their long, hard journey home through the snow. Polly smoked his after-dinner pipe, — the pipe was a hollow corn-cob with the tip of a buck's horn for a stem, — and the two bear hunters talked over the events of the day and discussed the coming campaign against the Fire Bear.

" I s'pose we'll have to hunt him by night,"

said Polly. " He's never seen at any other time, they say."

" Yes, we'll have to hunt him by night," said Balser; " but darkness will help us in the hunt, for we can see him better at night than at any other time, and he can't see us as well as he could in daylight."

" Balser, you surprise me," answered Polly. " Have you hunted bears all this time and don't know that a bear can see as well after night as in the daytime — better, maybe ? "

" Maybe that's so," responded Balser. " I know that cats and owls can see better by night, but I didn't know about bears. How do you know it's true ? "

" How do I know ? Why, didn't that there bear make a bee-line for this place last night, and wasn't last night as dark as the inside of a whale, and don't they go about at night more than in the daytime ? Tell me that. When do they steal sheep and shoats ? In daytime ? Tell me that. Ain't it always at night ? Did you ever hear of a bear stealing a shoat in the daytime ? No, sirree; but they can see the littlest shoat that ever grunted, on the darkest night, — see him and snatch him out of the pen and get away with him quicker than you or I could, a durned sight."

"I never tried; did you, Polly?" asked Balser.

Polly wasn't above suspicion among those who knew him, and Balser's question slightly disconcerted him.

"Well, I — I — durned if that ain't the worst fool question I ever heerd a boy ask," answered Polly. Then, somewhat anxious to change the conversation, he continued: —

"What night do you propose to come down here? To-morrow night?"

"No, not for a week. Not till seven nights after to-night," answered Balser, mindful of the charm which he hoped Liney's prayers would make for him.

"Seven nights? Geminy! I'm afraid I'll get scared of this place by that time. I'll bet this is an awful place at night; nothing but great chunks of blackness in these here gullies, so thick you could cut it with a knife. I'm not afraid now because I'm desperate. I'm so afraid of dyin' because I saw the Fire Bear that I don't seem to be afraid of nothin' else."

Polly was right. There is nothing like a counter-fear to keep a coward's courage up.

After they were warm and had rested, Balser and Polly went out of the cave and took another survey of the surrounding country from the top of the hill. They started homeward, and reached the cozy cabin on Blue River soon after sunset, tired, hungry, and cold. A good warm supper soon revived them, and as it had been agreed that Polly should remain at Mr. Brent's until after the Fire Bear hunt, they went to bed in the loft and slept soundly till morning.

After Balser announced his determination to hunt the Fire Bear, many persons asked him when he intended to undertake the perilous task, but the invariable answer he gave was, that he would begin after the seventh night from the one upon which the Fire Bear had visited Blue River. "Why after the seventh night?" was frequently asked; but the boy would give no other answer.

Balser had invited Tom Fox to go with him; and Tom, in addition to his redoubtable hatchet, intended to carry his father's gun. Polly would take Mr. Brent's rifle, and of course Balser would carry the greatest of all armaments, his smooth-bore carbine. Great were the preparations made in selecting bullets and in drying powder. Knives and hatchets were sharpened until they were almost as keen as a razor. Many of the men and boys of the neighbourhood volunteered to accompany Balser, but he would take with him no one but Tom and Polly.

"Too many hunters spoil the chase," said Balser, borrowing his thought from the cooks and the broth maxim.

Upon the morning of the eighth day Balser went over to see Liney, and to receive from her the precious charm redolent with forty-nine prayers from her pure heart. When she gave it to him he said: —

"It's a charm; I know it is." And he held it in his hand and looked at it affectionately. "It looks like a charm, and it feels like a charm. Liney, I seem to feel your prayers upon it."

"Ah! Balser, don't say that. It sounds almost wicked. It has seemed wicked all the time for me to try to make a charm."

"Don't feel that way, Liney. You didn't try to make it. You only prayed to God to make it, and God is good and loves to hear you pray. If He don't love to hear you pray, Liney, He don't love to hear any one."

"No, no, Balser, I'm so wicked. The night we saw the Fire Bear father read in the Bible where it says, 'The prayers of the wicked availeth not.' Oh, Balser, do you think it's wicked to try to make a charm — that is, to pray to God to make one?"

"No, indeed, Liney. God makes them

of His own accord. He made you." But Liney only half understood.

The charm worked at least one spell. It made the boy braver and gave him self-confidence.

Balser, Tom, and Polly had determined to ride down to Flatrock on horseback, and for that purpose one of Mr. Fox's horses and two of Mr. Brent's were brought into service. At three o'clock upon the famous eighth day the three hunters started for Flatrock, and spent the night in the vicinity of the mouth of Conn's Creek; but they did not see the Fire Bear. Four other expeditions were made, for Balser had no notion of giving up the hunt, and each expedition was a failure. But the fifth — well, I will tell you about it.

Upon the fifth expedition the boys reached Flatrock River just after sunset. A cold drizzling rain had begun to fall, and as it fell it froze upon the surface of the rocks. The wind blew and moaned through the tree-tops, and the darkness was so dense it seemed heavy. The boys had tied their horses in a cave, which they had used for the same purpose upon former visits, and were discussing the advisability of giving up the hunt for that night and returning home. Tom had suggested that the rain might extinguish the Fire Bear's fire so he could not be seen. The theory seemed plausible. Polly thought that a bear with any sense at all would remain at home in his cave upon such a night as that, and all these arguments, together with the slippery condition of the earth, which made walking among the rocks and cliffs very dangerous, induced Balser to conclude that it was best to return to Blue River without pursuing the hunt that night. He announced his decision, and had given up all hope of seeing the Fire Bear upon that expedition. But they were not to be disappointed after all, for, just as the boys were untying their horses to return home, a terrific growl greeted their ears, coming, it seemed, right from the mouth of the cave in which they stood.

"That's him," cried Polly. "I know his voice. I heerd it for one mortal hour that night when he was a chasin' me, and I'll never furgit it. I'd know it among a thousand bears. It's him. Oh, Balser, let's go home! For the Lord's sake, Balser, let's go home! I'd rather die three months from now than now. Three months is a long time to live, after all."

"Polly, what on earth are you talking about? Are you crazy? Tie up your horse at once," said Balser. "If the bear gets away from us this time, we'll never have another chance at him. Quick! Quick!"

Polly's courage was soon restored, and the horses were quickly tied again.

Upon entering the cave a torch had been lighted, and by the light of the torch, which Polly held, the primings of the guns were examined, knives and hatchets were made ready for immediate use, and out the hunters sallied in pursuit of the Fire Bear.

On account of the ice upon the rocks

it was determined that Polly should carry the torch with him. Aside from the dangers of the slippery path, there was another reason for carrying the torch. Fire attracts the attention of wild animals, and often prevents them from running away from the hunter. This is especially true of deer. So Polly carried the torch, and a fatal burden it proved to be for him. After the hunters had emerged from the cave, they at once started toward the river, and upon passing a little spur of the hill they beheld at a distance of two or three hundred yards the Fire Bear, glowing like a fiery heap against the black bank of night. He was running rapidly up the stream toward Black Gully, which came down to the river's edge between high cliffs. This was the place I described to you a few pages back. Balser and Polly had seen Black Gully before, and had noticed how dark, deep, and forbidding it was. It had seemed to them to be a fitting place for the revels of witches, demons, snakes, and monsters of all sorts and they thought surely it was haunted, if any place ever was. They feared the spot even in the daytime.

Polly, who was ingenious with a pocket-knife, had carved out three whistles, and in the bowl of each was a pea. These whistles produced a shrill noise when blown upon, which could be heard at a great distance, and each hunter carried one fastened to a string about his neck. In case the boys should be separated, one long whistle was to be sounded for the purpose of bringing them together; three whistles should mean that the bear had been seen, and one short one was to be the cry for help. When Balser saw the bear he blew a shrill blast upon his whistle to attract the brute's attention. The ruse produced the desired effect, for the bear stopped. His curiosity evidently was aroused by the noise and by the sight of the fire, and he remained standing for a moment or two while the boys ran forward as rapidly as the slippery rocks would permit. Soon they were within a hundred yards of the bear; then fifty forty, thirty, twenty. Still the Fire Bear did not move. His glowing form stood before them like a pillar of fire, the only object that could be seen in the darkness that surrounded him. He seemed to be the incarnation of all that was brave and demoniac. When within twenty yards of the bear Balser said hurriedly to his companions : —

"Halt! I'll shoot first, and you fellows hold your fire and shoot one at a time, after me. Don't shoot till I tell you, and take good aim. Polly, I'll hold your torch when I want you to shoot." Polly held the torch in one hand and his gun in the other, and fear was working great havoc with his usefulness. Balser continued : "It's so dark we can't see the sights of our guns, and if we're not careful we may all miss the bear, or still worse, we may only wound him. Hold up the torch, Polly, so I can see the sights of my gun."

Balser's voice seemed to attract the bear's

attention more even than did the torch, and he pricked up his short fiery ears as if to ask, " What are you talking about ? " When Balser spoke next it was with a tongue of fire, and the words came from his gun. The bear seemed to understand the gun's language better than that of Balser, for he gave forth in answer a terrific growl of rage, and bit savagely at the wound which Balser had inflicted. Alas! It was only a wound; for Balser's bullet, instead of piercing the bear's heart, had hit him upon the hind quarters.

" I've only wounded him," cried Balser, and the note of terror in his voice seemed to create a panic in the breasts of Tom and Polly, who at once raised their guns and fired. Of course they both missed the bear, and before they could lower their guns the monster was upon them.

Balser was in front, and received the full force of the brute's ferocious charge. The boy went down under the bear's mighty rush, and before he had time to draw his knife, or to disengage his hatchet from his belt, the infuriated animal was standing over him. As Balser fell his hand caught a rough piece of soft wood which was lying upon the ground, and with this he tried to beat the bear upon the head. The bear, of course, hardly felt the blows which Balser dealt with the piece of wood, and it seemed that another terrible proof was about to be given of the fatal consequences of looking upon the Fire Bear. Tom and Polly had both run when the bear charged, but Tom quickly came to Balser's relief, while Polly remained at a safe distance. The bear was reaching for Balser's throat, but by some fortunate chance he caught between his jaws the piece of wood with which Balser had been vainly striking him; and doubtless thinking that the wood was a part of Balser, the bear bit it and shook it ferociously. When Tom came up to the scene of conflict he struck the bear upon the head with the sharp edge of his hatchet, and chopped out one of his eyes. The pain of the wound seemed to double the bear's fury, and he sprang over Balser's prostrate form toward Tom. The bear rose upon his haunches and faced Tom, who manfully struck at him with his hatchet, and never thought of running. Ah! Tom was a brave one when the necessity for bravery arose. But Tom's courage was better than his judgment, for in a moment he was felled to the ground by a stroke from the bear's paw, and the bear was standing over him, growling and bleeding terribly. Polly had come nearer and his torch threw a ghastly glamour over the terrible scene. As in the fight with Balser, the bear tried to catch Tom's throat between his jaws; but here the soft piece of wood which Balser had grasped when he fell proved a friend indeed, for the bear had bitten it so savagely that his teeth had been embedded in its soft fibre, and it acted as a gag in his mouth. He could neither open nor close his jaws. After a few frantic efforts to bite Tom, the bear seemed to discover where the trouble was, and tried to push the wood out of his mouth with his paws. This gave Tom

a longed-for opportunity, of which he was
not slow to take advantage, and he quickly
drew himself from under the bear, rose to
his feet, and ran away. In the meantime
Balser rose from the ground and reached the
bear just as Tom started to run. Balser
knew by that time that he had no chance of
success in a hand-to-hand conflict with the
brute. So he struck the bear a blow upon
the head with his hatchet as he passed,
and followed Tom at a very rapid speed.
Balser at once determined that he and Tom
and Polly should reach a place of safety,
quickly load their guns, and return to the
attack. In a moment he looked back, and
saw the bear still struggling to free his
mouth from the piece of wood which had
saved two lives that night. As the bear was
not pursuing them, Balser concluded to halt;
and he and Tom loaded their guns, while
Polly held the torch on high to furnish light.
Polly's feeble wits had almost fled, and he
seemed unconscious of what was going on
about him. He did mechanically whatever

Balser told him to do, but his eyes had a far-away look, and it was evident that the events of the night had paralyzed his poor, weak brain. When the guns were loaded Balser and Tom hurried forward toward the bear, and poor Polly followed, bearing his torch. Bang! went Balser's gun, and the bear rose upon his hind feet, making the cliffs and ravines echo with his terrible growls.

"Take good aim, Tom; hold up the torch, Polly," said Balser. "Fire!" and the bear fell over on his back and seemed to be dead. Polly and Tom started toward the bear, but Balser cried out: "Stop! He may not be dead yet. We'll give him another volley. We've got him now, sure, if we're careful." Tom and Polly stopped, and it was fortunate for them that they did so; for in an instant the bear was on his feet, apparently none the worse for the ill-usage the boys had given him. The Fire Bear stood for a little time undetermined whether to attack the boys again or to run. After halting for a mo-ment between two opinions, he concluded to retreat, and with the piece of wood still in his mouth, he started at a rapid gait toward Black Gully, a hundred yards away.

"Load, Tom; load quick. Hold the torch, Polly," cried Balser. And again the guns were loaded, while poor demented Polly held the torch.

The bear moved away rapidly, and in a moment the boys were following him with loaded guns. When the brute reached the mouth of Black Gully he entered it. Evidently his home was in that uncanny place.

"Quick, quick, Polly!" cried Balser; and within a moment after the bear had entered Black Gully his pursuers were at the mouth of the ravine, making ready for another attack. Balser gave a shrill blast upon his whistle, and the bear turned for a moment, and deliberately sat down upon his haunches not fifty yards away. The place looked so black and dismal that the boys at first feared to enter, but soon their courage came to their rescue, and they marched in, with Polly in the lead. The bear moved farther up the gully toward an overhanging cliff, whose dark, rugged outlines were faintly illumined by the light of Polly's torch. The jutting rocks seemed like monster faces, and the bare roots of the trees were like the horny fingers and the bony arms of fiends. The boys followed the bear, and when he came to a halt near the cliff and again sat upon his haunches, it was evident that the Fire Bear's end was near at hand. How frightful it all appeared! There sat the Fire Bear, like a burning demon, sullen and motionless, giving forth, every few seconds, deep guttural growls that reverberated through the dark cavernous place. Not a star was seen, nor a gleam of light did the overcast sky afford. There stood poor, piteous Polly, all his senses fled and gone, unconsciously holding his torch above his head. The light of the torch seemed to give life to the shadows of the place, and a sense of fear stole over Balser that he could not resist

"Let's shoot him again, and get out of this awful place," said Balser

"You bet I'm willing to get out," said Tom, his teeth chattering, notwithstanding his wonted courage.

"Hold the torch, Polly," cried Balser, and Polly raised the torch. The boys were within fifteen yards of the bear, and each took deliberate aim and fired. The bear moaned and fell forward. Then Balser and Tom started rapidly toward the mouth of the gully. When they had almost reached the opening they looked back for Polly, who they thought was following them, but there he stood where they had left him, a hundred yards behind them.

Balser called, "Polly! Polly!" but Polly did not move. Then Tom blew his whistle, and Polly started, not toward them, alas! but toward the bear.

"Don't go to him, Polly," cried Balser. "He may not be dead. We've had enough of him to-night, for goodness' sake! We'll come back to-morrow and find him dead." But Polly continued walking slowly toward the bear.

"Polly! Polly! Come back!" cried both the boys. But Polly by that time was within ten feet of the bear, holding his torch and moving with the step of one unconscious of what he was doing. A few steps more and Polly was by the side of the terrible Fire Bear. The bear revived for a moment, and seemed conscious that an enemy was near him. With a last mighty effort he rose to his feet and struck Polly a blow with his paw which felled him to the ground. When Polly fell, the Fire Bear fell upon him, and Balser and Tom started to rescue their unfortunate friend. Then it was that a terrible thing happened. When Polly's torch dropped from his hand a blue flame three or four feet in height sprang from the ground just beyond the bear. The fire ran upon the ground for a short distance like a serpent of flame, and shot like a flash of chain lightning half-way up the side of the cliff. The dark, jutting rocks — huge demon faces covered with ice — glistened in the light of the blaze, and the

place seemed to have been transformed into
a veritable genii's cavern. The flames sank
away for a moment with a low, moaning
sound, and then came up again the colour of
roses and of blood. A great rumbling noise
was heard coming from the bowels of the
earth, and a tongue of fire shot twenty feet
into the air. This was more than flesh
and blood could endure, and Balser and
Tom ran for their lives, leaving their poor,
demented friend behind them to perish.
Out the boys went through the mouth of
the gully, and across the river they sped
upon the ice. They felt the earth tremble
beneath their feet, and they heard the
frightful rumbling again; then a loud explosion, like the boom of a hundred can-
nons, and the country for miles around
was lighted as if by the mid-day sun. Then
they looked back and beheld a sight which
no man could forget to the day of his
death. They saw a bright red flame a
hundred yards in diameter and two hundred
feet high leap from the Black Gully above

the top of the cliffs. After a moment great rocks, and pieces of earth half as large as a house, began to fall upon every side of them, as if a mighty volcano had burst forth; and the boys clung to each other in fear and trembling, and felt sure that judgment day had come.

After the rocks had ceased to fall, the boys, almost dead with fright, walked a short distance down the river and crossed upon the ice. The fire was still burning in the Black Gully, and there was no need of Polly's torch to help them see the slippery path among the rocks.

The boys soon found the cave in which the horses were stabled. They lost no time in mounting, and quickly started home, leading between them the horse which had been ridden by Polly. Poor Polly was never seen again. Even after the fire in the Black Gully had receded into the bowels of the earth whence it had come, nothing was found of his body nor that of the Fire Bear. They had each been burned to cinder.

Many of the Blue River people did not believe that the Fire Bear derived its fiery appearance from supernatural causes. They suggested that the bear probably had made its bed of decayed wood containing foxfire, and that its fur was covered with phosphorus which glowed like the light of the firefly after night. The explosion was caused by a "pocket" of natural gas which became ignited when Polly's torch fell to the ground by the side of the Fire Bear.

CHAPTER IX.

ON THE STROKE OF NINE.

LATE one afternoon — it was the day
before Christmas — Balser and Jim were
seated upon the extra backlog in the fireplace, ciphering. Mrs. Brent was sitting
in front of the fire in a rude home-made
rocking-chair, busily knitting, while she
rocked the baby's cradle with her foot and
softly sang the refrain of " Annie Laurie"
for a lullaby. Snow had begun to fall at
noon, and as the sun sank westward the
north wind came in fitful gusts at first, and
then in stronger blasts, till near the hour
of four, when Boreas burst forth in the
biting breath of the storm. How he howled
and screamed down the chimney at his
enemy, the fire! And how the fire crackled
and spluttered and laughed in the face of his

wrath, and burned all the brighter because of his raging! Don't tell me that a fire can't talk! A fire upon a happy hearth is the sweetest conversationalist on earth, and Boreas might blow his lungs out ere he could stop the words of cheer and health and love and happiness which the fire spoke to Jim and Balser and their mother in the gloaming of that cold and stormy day.

"Put on more wood," said the mother, in a whisper, wishing not to awaken the baby. "Your father will soon be home from Brookville, and we must make the house good and warm for him. I hope he will come early. It would be dreadful for him to be caught far away from home in such a storm as we shall have to-night."

Mr. Brent had gone to Brookville several days before with wheat and pelts for market, and was expected home that evening. Balser had wanted to go with his father, but the manly little fellow had given up his wish and had remained at home that he might take care of his mother, Jim, and the baby.

Balser quietly placed a few large hickory sticks upon the fire, and then whispered to Jim: —

" Let's go out and feed the stock and fix them for the night."

So the boys went to the barnyard and fed the horses and cows, and drove the sheep into the shed, and carried fodder from the huge stack and placed it against the north sides of the barn and shed to keep the wind from blowing through the cracks and to exclude the snow. When the stock was comfortable, cozy, and warm, the boys milked the cows, and brought to the house four bucketfuls of steaming milk, which they strained and left in the kitchen, rather than in the milk-house, that it might not freeze over night.

Darkness came on rapidly, and Mrs. Brent grew more and more anxious for her husband's return. Fearing that he might be late, she postponed supper until Jim's ever

ready appetite began to cry aloud for satisfaction, and Balser intimated that he, too,
might be induced to eat. So their mother
leisurely went to work to get supper, while
the baby was left sleeping before the cheery,
talkative fire in the front room.

A fat wild turkey roasted to a delicious
brown upon the spit, eggs fried in the
sweetest of lard, milk warm from the cows,
corn-cakes floating in maple syrup and yellow butter, sweet potatoes roasted in hot
ashes, and a great slice of mince pie furnished
a supper that makes one hungry but to think
about it. The boys, however, were hungry
without thinking, and it would have done
your heart good to see that supper disappear.

As they sat at supper they would pause
in their eating and listen attentively to
every noise made by the creaking of the
trees or the falling of a broken twig, hoping
that it was the step of the father. But the
supper was finished all too soon, and the
storm continued to increase in its fury;

the snow fell thicker and the cold grew fiercer, still Mr. Brent did not come.

Mrs. Brent said nothing, but as the hours flew by her anxious heart imparted its trouble to Balser, and he began to fear for his father's safety. The little clock upon the rude shelf above the fireplace hoarsely and slowly drawled out the hour of seven, then eight, and then nine. That was very late for the Brent family to be out of bed, and nothing short of the anxiety they felt could have kept them awake. Jim, of course, had long since fallen asleep, and he lay upon a soft bear-skin in front of the fire, wholly unconscious of storms or troubles of any sort. Mrs. Brent sat watching and waiting while Jim and the baby slept, and to her anxious heart it seemed that the seconds lengthened into minutes, and the minutes into hours, by reason of her loneliness. While she rocked beside the baby's cradle, Balser was sitting in his favourite place upon the backlog next to the fire. He had been reading, or trying to read, " The Pilgrim's Progress,' but visions of his father and of the team lost in the trackless forest, facing death by freezing, to say nothing of wolves that prowled the woods in packs of hundreds upon such a night as that, continually came between his eyes and the page, and blurred the words until they held no meaning. Gradually drowsiness stole over him, too, and just as the slow-going clock began deliberately to strike the hour of nine his head fell back into a little corner made by projecting logs in the wall of the fireplace, and, like Jim, he forgot his troubles as he slept.

Balser did not know how long he had been sleeping when the neighing of a horse was heard. Mrs. Brent hastened to the door, but when she opened it, instead of her husband she found one of the horses, an intelligent, raw-boned animal named Buck, standing near the house. Balser had heard her call, and he quickly ran out of doors and went to the horse. The harness was broken, and dragging upon the ground behind the horse were small portions of the wreck of the wagon.   Poor Buck's flank was red with blood, and his legs showed all too plainly the marks of deadly conflict with a savage, hungry foe.   The wreck of the wagon, the broken harness, and the wounds upon the

horse told eloquently, as if spoken in words, the story of the night.   Wolves had attacked Balser's father, and Buck had come home to give the alarm.

Balser ran quickly to the fire pile upon the hill and kindled it for the purpose of calling help from the neighbours.   Then he went back to the house and took down his gun.

He tied a bundle of torches over his shoulder, lighted one, and started out in the blinding, freezing storm to help his father, if possible.

He followed the tracks of the horse, which with the aid of his torch were easily discernible in the deep snow, and soon he was far into the forest, intent upon his mission of rescue.

After the boy had travelled for an hour he heard the howling of wolves, and hastened in the direction whence the sound came, feeling in his heart that he would find his father surrounded by a ferocious pack. He hurried forward as rapidly as he could run, and his worst fears were realized.

Soon he reached the top of a hill overlooking a narrow ravine which lay to the eastward. The moon had risen and the snow had ceased to fall. The wind was blowing a fiercer gale than ever, and had broken rifts in the black bank of snowcloud, so that gleams of the moon now and then enabled Balser's vision to penetrate the dark·

ness.   Upon looking down into the ravine
he beheld his father standing in the wagon,
holding in his hand a singletree which he
used as a weapon of defence.   The wolves

jumped upon the wagon in twos and threes,
and when beaten off by Mr. Brent would
crowd around the wheels and howl to get
their courage up, and renew the attack.

Mr. Brent saw the boy starting down the
hill toward the wagon and motioned to him
to go back.   Balser quickly perceived that
it would be worse than madness to go to his

father. The wolves would at once turn their attack upon him, and his father would be compelled to abandon his advantageous position in the wagon and go to his relief, in which case both father and son would be lost. Should Balser fire into the pack of wolves from where he stood, he would bring upon himself and his father the same disaster. He felt his helplessness grievously, but his quick wit came to his assistance. He looked about him for a tree which he could climb, and soon found one. At first he hesitated to make use of the tree, for it was dead and apparently rotten; but there was none other at hand, so he hastily climbed up and seated himself firmly upon a limb which seemed strong enough to sustain his weight.

Balser was now safe from the wolves, and at a distance of not more than twenty yards from his father. There he waited until the clouds for a moment permitted the full light of the moon to rest upon the scene, and then he took deliberate aim and fired into the pack of howling wolves. A sharp yelp answered his shot, and then a black, seething mass of growling, fighting, snapping beasts fell upon the carcass of the wolf that Balser's shot had killed, and almost instantly they devoured their unfortunate companion.

Balser felt that if he could kill enough wolves to satisfy the hunger of the living ones they would abandon their attack upon his father, for wolves, like cowardly men, are brave only in desperation. They will attack neither man nor animal except when driven to do so by hunger.

After Balser had killed the wolf, clouds obscured the moon before he could make another shot. He feared to fire in the dark lest he might kill his father, so he waited impatiently for the light which did not come.

Meanwhile, the dead wolf having been devoured, the pack again turned upon Mr. Brent, and Balser could hear his father's voice and the clanking of the iron upon the singletree as he struck at the wolves to ward them off.

It seemed to Balser that the moon had

gone under the clouds never to appear again.
Mr. Brent continually called loudly to the
wolves, for the human voice is an awesome
sound even to the fiercest animals. To Balser the tone of his father's voice, mingled
with the howling of wolves, was a note of
desperation that almost drove him frantic.
The wind increased in fury every moment,
and Balser felt the cold piercing to the mar-
row of his bones. He had waited it seemed
to him hours for the light of the moon again
to shine, but the clouds appeared to grow
deeper and the darkness more dense.

While Balser was vainly endeavouring to
watch the conflict at the wagon, he heard
a noise at the root of the tree in which
he had taken refuge, and, looking down, he
discovered a black monster standing quietly
beneath him. It was a bear that had been
attracted to the scene of battle by the noise.
Balser at once thought, " Could I kill this
huge bear, his great carcass certainly would
satisfy the hunger of the wolves that sur-
round my father." Accordingly he lowered

". . . . IMAGINE HIS CONSTERNATION WHEN HE RECOGNIZED THE FORMS OF LINEY FOX AND HER BROTHER TOM."

the point of his gun, and, taking as good aim as the darkness would permit, he fired upon the bear. The bear gave forth a frightful growl of rage and pain, and as it did so its companion, a beast of enormous size, came running up, apparently for the purpose of rendering assistance.

Balser hastily reloaded his gun and prepared to shoot the other bear. This he soon did, and while the wolves howled about his father the two wounded bears at the foot of the tree made night hideous with their ravings.

Such a frightful bedlam of noises had never before been heard.

Balser was again loading his gun, hoping to finish the bears, when he saw two lighted torches approaching along the path over which he had just come, and as they came into view imagine his consternation when he recognized the forms of Liney Fox and her brother Tom. Tom carried his father's gun, for Mr. Fox had gone to Brookville, and Liney, in addition to her torch, carried

Tom's hatchet. Liney and Tom were ap·
proaching rapidly, and Balser called out to
them to stop. They did not hear him, or
did not heed him, but continued to go
forward to their death. The bears at the
foot of the tree were wounded, and would
be more dangerous than even the pack of
wolves howling at the wagon.

"Go back! Go back!" cried Balser des·
perately, "or you'll be killed. Two wounded
bears are at the root of the tree I'm in,
and a hundred wolves are howling in the
hollow just below me. Run for your lives!
Run! You'll be torn in pieces if you come
here."

The boy and girl did not stop, but con·
tinued to walk rapidly toward the spot from
which they had heard Balser call. The
clouds had drifted away from the moon,
and now that the light was of little use to
Balser — for he was intent upon saving
Liney and Tom — there was plenty of it.

The sound of his voice and the growling
of the bears had attracted the attention of

HE FELL A DISTANCE OF TEN OR TWELVE FEET, . . . AND LAY HALF STUNNED."

the wolves.   They were wavering in their attack upon Mr. Brent, and evidently had half a notion to fall upon the bears that Balser had wounded.   Meantime Liney and Tom continued to approach, and their torches, which under ordinary circumstances would have frightened the animals away, attracted the attention of the bears and the wolves, and drew the beasts upon them. They were now within a few yards of certain death, and again Balser in agony cried out: "Go back, Liney!   Go back!   Run for your lives!"   In his eagerness he rose to his feet, and took a step or two out upon the rotten limb on which he had been seated As he called to Liney and Tom, and motioned to them frantically to go back, the limb upon which he was standing broke, and he fell a distance of ten or twelve feet to the ground, and lay half stunned between the two wounded bears.   Just as Balser fell, Liney and Tom came up to the rotten tree, and at the same time the pack of wolves abandoned their attack upon Mr. Brent and rushed like a herd of howling demons upon the three helpless children.

One of the bears immediately seized Balser, and the other one struck Liney to the ground. By the light of the torches Mr. Brent saw all that had happened, and when the wolves abandoned their attack upon him he hurried forward to rescue Balser, Liney, and Tom, although in so doing he was going to meet his death. In a few seconds Mr. Brent was in the midst of the terrible fight, and a dozen wolves sprang upon him. Tom's gun was useless, so he snatched the hatchet from Liney, who was lying prostrate under one of the bears, and tried to rescue her from its jaws. Had he done so. however, it would have been only to save her for the wolves. But his attempt to rescue Liney was quickly brought to an end. The wolves sprang upon Tom, and soon he, too, was upon the ground. The resinous torches which had fallen from the hands of Tom and Liney continued to burn, and cast a lurid light upon the terrible scene.

Consciousness soon returned to Balser, and he saw with horror the fate that was in store for his father, his friends, and him- self. Despair took possession of his soul, and he knew that the lamp of life would soon be black in all of them forever. While his father and Tom lay upon the ground at the mercy of the wolves, and while Liney was lying within arm's reach of him in the jaws of the wounded bear, and he utterly helpless to save the girl of whom he was so fond, Balser's mother shook him by the shoulder and said, " Balser, your father is coming." Balser sprang to his feet, looked dazed for a moment, and then ran, half weeping, half laughing, into his father's arms . . . just as the sleepy little clock had finished striking nine.

CHAPTER IX.

A CASTLE ON THE BRANDYWINE

CHRISTMAS morning the boys awakened early and crept from beneath their warm bearskins in eager anticipation of gifts from Santa Claus. Of course they had long before learned who Santa Claus was, but they loved the story, and in the wisdom of their innocence clung to an illusion which brought them happiness.

The sun had risen upon a scene such as winter only can produce. Surely Aladdin had come to Blue River upon the wings of the Christmas storm, had rubbed his lamp, and lo! the humble cabin was in the heart of a fairyland such as was never conceived by the mind of a genie. Snow lay upon the ground like a soft carpet of white velvet ten inches thick. The boughs of the trees were festooned with a foliage that spring cannot rival. Even the locust trees, which in their pride of blossom cry out in June time for our admiration, seemed to say, " See what we can do in winter; " and the sycamore and beech drooped their branches, as if to call attention to their winter flowers given by that rarest of artists, Jack Frost.

The boys quickly donned their heavy buckskin clothing and moccasins, and climbed down the pole to the room where their father and mother were sleeping. Jim awakened his parents with a cry of " Christmas Gift," but Balser's attention was attracted to a barrel standing by the fireplace, which his father had brought from Brookville, and into which the boys had not been permitted to look the night before. Balser had a shrewd suspicion of what the barrel contained, and his delight knew no bounds when he found, as he had hoped, that it was filled with steel traps of the size used to catch beavers, coons, and foxes.

Since he had owned a gun, Balser's great desire had been to possess a number of traps. As I have already told you, the pelts of animals taken in winter are of great value, and our little hero longed to begin life on his own account as a hunter and trapper.

I might tell you of the joyous Christmas morning in the humble cabin when the gifts which Mr. Brent had brought from Brookville were distributed. I might tell you of the new gown for mother, of the bright, red mufflers, of the shoes for Sunday wear and the "store" caps for the boys, to be used upon holiday occasions. I might tell you of the candies and nuts, and of the rarest of all the gifts, an orange for each member of the family, for that fruit had never before been seen upon Blue River. But I must take you to the castle on Brandywine.

You may wonder how there came to be a castle in the wilderness on Brandywine, but I am sure, when you learn about it, you will declare that it was fairer than any castle ever built of mortar and stone, and that the adventures which befell our little heroes were as glorious as ever fell to the lot of spurred and belted knight.

Immediately after breakfast, when the chores had all been finished, Balser and Jim started down the river to visit Liney and Tom. Balser carried with him two Christmas presents for his friends — a steel trap for Tom, and the orange which his father had brought him from Brookville for Liney.

I might also tell you of Tom's delight when he received the trap, and of Liney's smile of pleasure, worth all the oranges in the world, when she received her present; and I might tell you how she divided the orange into pieces, and gave one to each of the family; and how, after it had all been eaten, tears came to her bright eyes when she learned that Balser had not tasted the fruit. I might tell you much more that would be interesting, and show you how good and true and gentle were these honest, simple folk, but I must drop it all and begin my story.

Balser told Tom about the traps, and a trapping expedition was quickly agreed upon between the boys.

The next day Tom went to visit Balser,

and for three or four days the boys were
busily engaged in making two sleds upon
which to carry provisions for their campaign.
The sleds when finished were each about two
feet broad and six feet long. They were
made of elm, and were very strong, and
were so light that when loaded the boys
could easily draw them over the snow. By
the time the sleds were finished the snow
was hard, and everything was ready for the
moving of the expedition.

First, the traps were packed. Then provisions, consisting of sweet potatoes, a great
lump of maple sugar, a dozen loaves of white
bread, two or three gourds full of butter, a
side of bacon, a bag of meal, a large piece of
bear meat for the dogs, and a number of
other articles and simple utensils such as the
boys would need in cooking, were loaded
upon the sleds. They took with them no
meat other than bacon and the bear meat
for the dogs, for they knew they could
make traps from the boughs of trees in
which they could catch quail and pheas-

ants, and were sure to be able, in an hour's
hunting, to provide enough venison to supply their wants for a much longer time than
they would remain in camp. There were
also wild turkeys to be killed, and fish to be
caught through openings which the boys
would make in the ice of the creek.

Over the loaded sleds they spread woolly
bearskins to be used for beds and covering
during the cold nights, and they also took
with them a number of tanned deerskins,
with which to carpet the floor of their castle
and to close its doors and windows. Tom
took with him his wonderful hatchet, an axe,
and his father's rifle. Axe, hatchets, and
knives had been sharpened, and bullets had
been moulded in such vast numbers that one
would have thought the boys were going to
war. Powder horns were filled, and a can
of that precious article was placed carefully
upon each of the sleds.

Bright and early one morning Balser,
Tom, and Jim, and last, but by no means
least, Tige and Prince, crossed Blue River

and started in a northwestern direction toward a point on Brandywine where a number of beaver dams were known to exist, ten miles distant from the Brent cabin.

EN ROUTE FOR THE CASTLE.

Tom and Tige drew one of the sleds, and Balser and Prince drew the other. During the first part of the trip, Jim would now and then lend a helping hand, but toward the latter end of the journey he said he thought it would be better for him to ride upon one of the sleds to keep the load from fall

ing off. Balser and Tom, however, did
not agree with him, nor did the dogs; so
Jim walked behind and grumbled, and had
his grumbling for his pains, as usually is the
case with grumblers.

Two or three hours before sunset the boys
reached Brandywine, a babbling little creek in
springtime, winding its crooked rippling way
through overhanging boughs of water elm,

sycamore, and willows, but, at the time of our
heroes' expedition, frozen over with the mail
of winter. It is in small creeks, such as Brandywine, that beavers love to make their dams.

Our little caravan, upon reaching Brandywine, at once took to the ice and started up-
stream along its winding course.

Jim had grown tired. "I don't believe

you fellows know where you're going," said
he. " I don't see any place to camp."

" You'll see it pretty quickly," said Balser;
and when they turned a bend in the creek
they beheld a huge sycamore springing from a
little valley that led down to the water's edge.

" There's our home," said Balser.

The sycamore was hollow, and at its roots
was an opening for a doorway.

Upon beholding the tree Jim gave a cry of
delight, and was for entering their new home
at once, but Balser held him back and sent
in the dogs as an exploring advance guard.
Soon the dogs came out and informed the
boys that everything within the tree was all
right, and Balser and Tom and Jim stooped
low and entered upon the possession of their
castle on Brandywine.

The first task was to sweep out the dust
and dry leaves. This the boys did with bun-
dles of twigs rudely fashioned into brooms.
The dry leaves and small tufts of black hair
gave evidence all too strongly that the castle
which the boys had captured was the home of

some baron bear who had incautiously left his stronghold unguarded. Jim spoke of this fact with unpleasant emphasis, and was ready to "bet" that the bear would come back when they were all asleep, and would take possession of his castle and devour the intruders.

"*What* will you bet?" said Tom.

"I didn't say I would bet anything. I just said I'd bet, and you'll see I'm right," returned Jim.

Balser and Tom well knew that Jim's prophecy might easily come true, but they had faith in the watchfulness of their sentinels, Tige and Prince, and the moon being at its full, they hoped rather than feared that his bearship might return, and were confident that, in case he did, his danger would be greater than theirs.

After the castle floor had been carefully swept, the boys carried in the deerskins and spread them on the ground for a carpet. The bearskins were then taken in, and the beds were made ; traps, guns, and provisions were stored away, and the sleds were drawn around to one side of the door, and placea leaning against the tree.

The boys were hungry, and Jim insisted that supper should be prepared at once; but Tom, having made several trips around the tree, remarked mysteriously that he had a plan of his own. He said there was a great deal of work to be done before sundown, and that supper could be eaten after dark when they could not work. Tom was right, for the night gave promise of bitter cold.

Limpy did not tell his plans at once, but soon they were developed.

The hollow in the tree in which the boys had made their home was almost circular in form. It was at least ten or eleven feet in diameter, and extended up into the tree twenty or thirty feet. Springing from the same root, and a part of the parent tree, grew two large sprouts or branches, which at a little distance looked like separate trees. They were, however, each connected with the larger tree, and the three formed one.

" What on earth are you pounding at that

tree for?" asked Jim, while Tom was striking one of the smaller trees with the butt end of the hatchet, and listening inte tly as if he expected to hear a response.

Tom did not reply to Jim, but in a moment entered the main tree with axe in hand, and soon Balser and Jim heard him chopping.

The two boys at once followed Tom, to learn what their eccentric companion was doing. Tom did not respond to their questions, but after he had chopped vigorously for a few minutes the result of his work gave them an answer, for he soon cut an opening into the smaller tree, which was also hollow. Tom had discovered the hollow by striking the tree with his hatchet. In fact, Tom was a genius after his own peculiar pattern.

The newly discovered hollow proved to be three or four feet in diameter, and, like that in the larger tree, extended to a considerable height. After Tom had made the opening between the trees, he sat upon the ground, and with his hatchet hewed it to an oval shape, two feet high and two feet broad.

Jim could not imagine why Tom had taken so much trouble to add another room to their house, which was already large enough. But when Tom, having finished the opening upon the inside, went out and began to climb the smaller tree with the help of a few low-growing branches, the youngest member of the expedition became fully convinced in his own mind that the second in command was out of his head entirely. When Tom, having climbed to a height of twelve or fifteen feet, began to chop with his hatchet, Jim remarked, in most emphatic language, that he thought " a fellow who would chop at a sycamore tree just for the sake of making chips, when he might be eating his supper, was too big a fool to live."

Tom did not respond to Jim's sarcasm, but persevered in his chopping until he had made an opening at the point to which he had climbed. Balser had quickly guessed the object of Tom's mighty labors, but he did not enlighten Jim. He had gone to other work, and by the time Tom had made the opening from the outside of the smaller tree, had collected a pile of firewood, and had carried several loads of it into the castle. Then Tom came down, and Jim quickly followed him into the large tree, for by that time his mysterious movements were full of interest to the little fellow.

Now what do you suppose was Tom's object in wasting so much time and energy with his axe and hatchet?

A fireplace.

You will at once understand that the opening which Tom had cut in the tree at the height of twelve or fifteen feet was for the purpose of making a chimney through which the smoke might escape.

The boys kindled a fire, and in a few minutes there was a cheery blaze in their fireplace that lighted up the room and made "everything look just like home," Jim said.

Then Jim went outside and gave a great hurrah of delight when he saw the smoke issuing from the chimney that ingenious Tom had made with his hatchet.

Jim watched the smoke for a few moments, and then walked around the tree to
survey the premises. The result of his
survey was the discovery of a hollow in

THE CASTLE ON THE BRANDYWINE.

the third tree of their castle, and when he
informed Balser and Tom of the important
fact, it was agreed that the room which
Jim had found should be prepared for Tige

and Prince. The dogs were not fastidious, and a sleeping-place was soon made for them entirely to their satisfaction.

Meantime the fire was blazing and crackling in the fireplace, and the boys began to prepare supper. They had not had time to kill game, so they fried a few pieces of bacon and a dozen eggs, of which they had brought a good supply, and roasted a few sweet potatoes in the ashes. Then they made an opening in the ice, from which they drew a bucketful of sparkling ice water, and when all was ready they sat down to supper, served with the rarest of all dressings, appetite sauce, and at least one of the party, Jim, was happy as a boy could be.

The dogs then received their supper of bear meat.

The members of the expedition, from the commanding officer Balser to the high privates Tige and Prince, were very tired after their hard day's work, and when Tom and Balser showed the dogs their sleeping-place they curled up close to each other and soon were in the land of dog dreams.

By the time supper was finished night had fallen, and while Tom and Balser were engaged in stretching a deerskin across the door to exclude the cold air, Jim crept between the bearskins and soon was sound asleep, dreaming no doubt of suppers and dinners and breakfasts, and scolding in his dreams like the veritable little grumbler that he was. A great bed of embers had accumulated in the fireplace, and upon them Balser placed a hickory knot for the purpose of retaining fire till morning, and then he covered the fire with ashes.

After all was ready Balser and Tom crept in between the bearskins, and lying spoon-fashion, one on each side of Jim, lost no time in making a rapid, happy journey to the land of Nod.

Tom slept next to the wall, next to Tom lay Jim, and next to Jim was Balser. The boys were lying with their feet to the fire, and upon the opposite side of the room was the doorway closed by the deerskin, of which I have already told you.

Of course they went to bed "all standing," as sailors say when they lie down to sleep with their clothing on, for the weather was cold, and the buckskin clothing and moccasins were soft and pleasant to sleep in, and would materially assist the bearskins in keeping the boys warm.

It must have been a pretty sight in the last flickering light of the smouldering fire to see the three boys huddled closely together, covered by the bearskins. I have no doubt had you seen them upon that night they would have appeared to you like a sleeping bear. In fact, before the night was over they did appear to — but I must not go ahead of my story.

The swift-winged hours of darkness sped like moments to the sleeping boys. The smouldering coals in the fireplace were black and lustreless. The night wind softly moaned through the branches of the sycamore, and sighed as it swept the bare limbs of the willows and the rustling tops of the underbrush. Jack Frost was silently at work, and the cold, clear air seemed to glitter in the moonlight. It was an hour past midnight. Had the boys been awake and listening, or had Tige and Prince been attending to their duties as sentinels, they would have heard a crisp noise of footsteps, as the icy surface of the snow cracked, and as dead twigs broke beneath a heavy weight. Ah, could the boys but awaken! Could the dogs be aroused but for one instant from their deep lethargy of slumber!

Balser! Tom! Jim! Tige! Prince! Awaken! Awaken!

On comes the heavy footfall, cautiously. As it approaches the castle a few hurried steps are taken, and the black, awkward form lifts his head and sniffs the air for signs of danger.

The baron has returned to claim his own, and Jim's prophecy, at least in part, has come true. The tracks upon the snow left by the boys and dogs, and the sleds leaning against the tree, excite the bear's suspicion, and he stands like a statue for five minutes, trying to make up his mind whether or not he shall enter his old domain. The memory of his cozy home tempts him, and he cautiously walks to the doorway of his house. The deerskin stretched across the opening surprises him, and he carefully examines it with the aid of his chief counsellor, his nose. Then he thrusts it aside with his head and enters.

He sees the boys on the opposite side of the tree, and doubtless fancies that his mate has gotten home before him, so he complacently lies down beside the bearskins, and soon, he, too, is in the land of bear dreams.

When a bear sleeps he snores, and the first loud snort from the baron's nostrils aroused Balser. At first Balser's mind was in confusion, and he thought that he was at home. In a moment, however, he remembered where he was, and waited in the darkness for a repetition of the sound that had awakened him. Soon it came again, and Balser in his drowsiness fancied that Tom had changed his place and was lying beside him, though never in all his life had he heard such sounds proceed from Limpy's nose. So he reached out his hand, and at once was undeceived, for he touched the bear, and at last Balser was awake. The boy's hair seemed to stand erect upon his head, and his blood grew cold in his veins, as he realized the terrible situation. All was darkness. The guns, hatchets, and knives were upon the opposite side of the tree, and to reach them or to reach the doorway Balser would have to climb over the bear. Cold as the night was, perspiration sprang from every pore of his skin, and terror took possession of him such as he had never before known. It seemed a long time that he lay there, but it could not have been more than a few seconds until the bear gave forth another snort, and Tom raised up from his side of the bed, and said: " Balser, for goodness' sake stop snoring. The noise you make would bring a dead man to life."

Tom's voice aroused the bear, and it immediately rose upon its haunches with a deep growl that seemed to shake the tree. Then Jim awakened and began to scream. At the same instant Tige and Prince entered the tree, and a fight at once ensued between the bear and dogs. The bear was as badly frightened as the boys, and when it and the dogs ran about the room the boys were thrown to the ground and trampled upon.

The beast, in his desperate effort to escape, ran into the fireplace and scattered the coals and ashes. As he could not escape through the fireplace, he backed into the room, and again made the rounds of the tree with the dogs at his heels. Again the boys were knocked about as if they were ninepins. They made an effort to reach the door, but all I have told you about took place so quickly, and the darkness was so intense, that they failed to escape. Meantime the fight between the dogs and the bear went on furiously, and the barking, yelping, growling, and snarling made a noise that was deafening. Balser lifted Jim to his arms and tried to save him from injury, but his efforts were of small avail, for with each plunge of the bear the boys were thrown to the ground or dashed against the tree, until it seemed that there was not a spot upon their bodies that was not bruised and scratched. At last, after a minute or two of awful struggle and turmoil — a minute or two that seemed hours to the boys — the bear made his exit through the door followed closely by Tige and Prince, who clung to him with a persistency not to be shaken off.

You may be sure that the boys lost no time in making their exit also. Their first thoughts, of course, were of each other, and when Balser learned that Jim and Tom had received no serious injury, he quickly turned his head in the direction whence the bear and dogs had gone, and saw them at a point in the bend of the creek not fifty yards away. The bear had come to bay, and the dogs were in front of him, at a safe distance, barking furiously, Then Balser's courage returned, and he hastily went into the tree, brought out his carbine, and hurried toward the scene of conflict. The moon was at its full, and the snow upon the trees and upon the ground helped to make the night almost as light as day. The bear was sitting erect upon his haunches, hurling defiant growls at the dogs, and when Balser approached him, the brute presented his breast as a fair mark. Tom also fetched his gun and followed closely at Balser's heels. The attention of the bear was so occupied with the dogs that he gave no heed to the boys, and they easily approached him to within a distance of five or six yards. Tom and Balser stood for a moment or two with their guns ready to fire, and Balser said: "Tom, you shoot first. I'll watch carefully, and hold my fire until the bear makes a rush, should you fail to kill him."

Much to Balser's surprise, Tom quickly and fearlessly took three or four steps toward the bear, and when he lifted his father's long gun to fire, the end of it was within three yards of the bear's breast.

Balser held his ground, much frightened at Tom's reckless bravery, but did not dare to speak. When Tom fired, the bear gave forth a fearful growl, and sprang like a wildcat right upon the boy. Tom fell to the ground upon his back, and the bear stood over him. The dogs quickly made an attack, and Balser hesitated to fire, fearing that he might kill Tom or one of the dogs. Then came Jim, who rushed past Balser toward Tom and the bear, and if Jim's courage had ever before been doubted, all such doubts were upon that night removed forever. The little fellow carried in his hand Tom's hatchet, and without fear or hesitancy he ran to the bear and began to strike him with all his little might. Meantime poor, prostrate Tom was crying piteously for help, and, now that Jim was added to the group. it seemed impossible for Balser to fire at the bear. But no time was to be lost. If Bal-

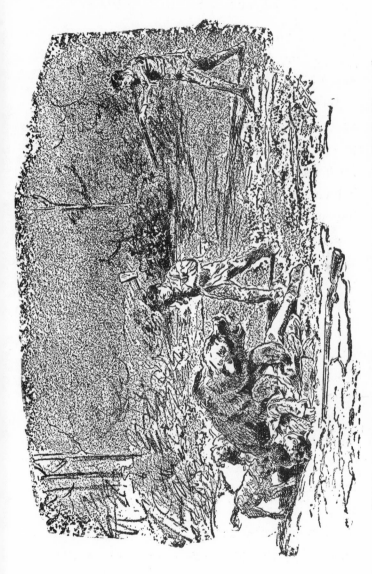

"BALSER HESITATED TO FIRE, FEARING THAT HE MIGHT KILL TOM OR ONE OF THE DOGS."

ser did not shoot, Tom certainly would be killed in less than ten seconds. So, without stopping to take thought, and upon the impulse of one of those rare intuitions under the influence of which persons move so accurately, Balser lifted his gun to his shoulder. He could see the bear's head plainly as it swayed from side to side, just over Tom's throat, and it seemed that he could not miss his aim. Almost without looking, he pulled the trigger. He felt the rebound of the gun and heard the report breaking the heavy silence of the night. Then he dropped the gun upon the snow and covered his face with his hands, fearing to see the result of his shot. He stood for a moment trembling. The dogs had stopped barking; the bear had stopped growling; Jim had ceased to cry out; Tom had ceased his call for help, and the deep silence rested upon Balser's heart like a load of lead. He could not take his hands from his face. After a moment he felt Jim's little hand upon his arm, and Tom said, as he drew himself from beneath the bear, " Balser, there's no man or boy living but you that could have made that shot in the moonlight."

Then Balser knew that he had killed the bear, and he sank upon the snow and wept as if his heart would break.

Notwithstanding the intense cold, the excitement of battle had made the boys unconscious of it, and Tom and Jim stood by Balser's side as he sat upon the snow, and they did not feel the sting of the night.

Poor little Jim, who was so given to grumbling, much to the surprise of his companions fell upon his knees, and said, " Don't cry, Balser, don't cry," although the tears were falling over the little fellow's own cheeks. " Don't cry any more, Balser, the bear is dead all over. I heard the bullet whiz past my ears, and I heard it strike the bear's head just as plain as you can hear that owl hoot; and then I knew that you had saved Tom and me, because nobody can shoot as well as you can."

The little fellow's tenderness and his

pride in Balser seemed all the sweeter, because it sprang from his childish gruffness.

Tom and Jim helped Balser to his feet,
and they went over to the spot where the
bear was lying stone dead with Balser's
bullet in his brain. The dogs were sniffing
at the dead bear, and the monster brute lay
upon the snow in the moonlight, and looked
like a huge incarnate fiend.

After examining him for a moment the
boys slowly walked back to the tree. When
they had entered they raked the coals together, put on an armful of wood, called in
the dogs to share their comfort, hung up the
deerskin at the door, drew the bearskins in
front of the fire, and sat down to talk and
think, since there was no sleep left in their
eyes for the rest of that night.

After a long silence Jim said, " I told you
he'd come back."

"But he didn't eat us," replied Tom,
determined that Jim should not be right in
everything.

"He'd have eaten you, Limpy Fox, if

Balser hadn't been the best shot in the world."

"That's what he would," answered Tom, half inclined to cry.

"Nonsense," said Balser, "anybody could have done it."

"Well, I reckon not," said Jim. "Me and Tom and the dogs and the bear was as thick as six in a bed; and honest, Balser, I think you had to shoot around a curve to miss us all but the bear."

After a few minutes Jim said: "Golly! wasn't that an awful fight we had in here before the bear got out?"

"Yes, it was," returned Balser, seriously.

"Well, I rather think it was," continued Jim. "Honestly, fellows, I ran around this here room so fast for a while, that — that I could see my own back most of the time."

Balser and Tom laughed, and Tom said: "Jim, if you keep on improving, you'll be a bigger liar than that fellow in the Bible before you're half his age."

Then the boys lapsed into silence, and the

dogs lay stretched before the fire till the welcome sun began to climb the hill of the
sky and spread his blessed tints of gray and
blue and pink and red, followed by the
glorious flood of day.

After breakfast the boys skinned the bear
and cut his carcass into small pieces — that
is, such portions of it as they cared to keep.
They hung the bearskin and meat upon the
branches of their castle beyond the reach of
wolves and foxes, and they gave to Tige and
Prince each a piece of meat that made their
sides stand out with fulness.

The saving of the bear meat and skin
consumed most of the morning, and at noon
the boys took a loin steak from the bear and
broiled it upon the coals for dinner. After
dinner they began the real work of the
expedition by preparing to set the traps.

When all was ready they started up the
creek, each boy carrying a load of traps over
his shoulder. At a distance of a little more
than half a mile from the castle they found a
beaver dam stretching across the creek, and

at the water's edge near each end of the dam
they saw numberless tracks made by the
little animals whose precious pelts they were
so anxious to obtain.

I should like to tell you of the marvellous
home of that wonderful little animal the
beaver, and of his curious habits and instincts; how he chops wood and digs into
the ground and plasters his home, under the
water, with mud, using his tail for shovel
and trowel.   But all that you may learn from
any book on natural history, and I assure
you it will be found interesting reading.

The boys placed five or six traps upon the
beaver paths on each side of the creek, and
then continued their journey up stream until
they found a little opening in the ice down
to which, from the bank above, ran a well-
beaten path, telling plainly of the many
kinds of animals that had been going there
to drink.   There they set a few traps and
baited them with small pieces of bear meat,
and then they returned home, intending
to visit the traps next morning at an early

hour, and hoping to reap a rich harvest of pelts.

When the boys reached home it lacked little more than an hour of sunset, but the young fellows had recovered from the excitement of the night before, which had somewhat destroyed their appetites for breakfast and dinner, and by the time they had returned from setting their traps those same appetites were asserting themselves with a vigour that showed plainly enough a fixed determination to make up for lost time.

" How would a wild turkey or a venison steak taste for supper ? " asked Balser.

Jim simply looked up at him with a greedy, hungry expression, and exclaimed the one word — " Taste ? "

" Well, I'll go down the creek a little way and see what I can find. You fellows stay here and build a fire, so that we can have a fine bed of coals when I return."

Balser shouldered his gun and went down the creek to find his supper. He did not take the dogs, for he hoped to kill a wild turkey, and dogs are apt to bark in the pursuit of squirrels and rabbits, thereby frightening the turkey, which is a shy and wary bird.

When the boy had travelled quite a long distance down stream, he began to fear

that, after all, he should be compelled to content himself with a rabbit or two for supper. So he turned homeward and scanned the woods carefully for the humble game, that he might not go home entirely empty-handed.

Upon his journey down the creek rabbits had sprung up on every side of him, but now that he wanted a pair for supper they all had mysteriously disappeared, and he feared that he and the boys and the dogs would be compelled to content themselves with bear meat.

When the boy was within a few hundred yards of home, and had almost despaired of obtaining even a rabbit, he espied a doe and a fawn, standing upon the opposite side of the creek at a distance of sixty or seventy yards, watching him intently with their

"ESPIED A DOE AND A FAWN, STANDING UPON THE OPPOSITE SIDE OF THE CREEK."

great brown eyes, so full of fatal curiosity. Balser imitated the cry of the fawn, and held the attention of the doe until he was enabled to lessen the distance by fifteen or twenty yards. Then he shot the fawn, knowing that if he did so, its mother, the doe. would run for a short distance and

would return to the fawn. In the meantime Balser would load his gun and would
kill the doe when she returned. And so it
happened that the doe and the fawn each
fell a victim to our hunter's skill. Balser
threw the fawn over his shoulder and carried it to the castle; then the boys took
one of the sleds and fetched home the doe.

They hung the doe high upon the branches
of the sycamore, and cut the fawn into small
pieces, which they put upon the ice of the
creek and covered with snow, that the
meat might quickly cool. The bed of coals
was ready, and the boys were ready too,
you may be sure.

Soon the fawn meat cooled, and soon each
boy was devouring a savoury piece that had
been broiled upon the coals.

After supper the boys again built a fine
fire, and sat before it talking of the events
of the day, and wondering how many beavers,
foxes, coons, and muskrats they would find
in their traps next morning.

As the fire died down drowsiness stole

over our trappeis, who were in the habit of going to bed soon after sunset, and they again crept in between the bearskins with Jim in the middle. They, however, took the precaution to keep Tige and Prince in the same room with them, and the boys slept that night without fear of an intrusion such as had disturbed them the night before.

Next morning, bright and early, the boys hurried up the creek to examine their traps, and greatly to their joy found five beavers and several minks, coons, and muskrats safely captured. Near one of the traps was the foot of a fox, which its possessor had bitten off in the night when he learned that he could not free it from the cruel steel.

The boys killed the animals they had caught by striking them on the head with a heavy club, which method of inflicting death did not damage the pelts as a sharp instrument or bullet would have done. After resetting the traps, our hunters placed the game upon the sled and hurried home to their castle, where the pelts were carefully removed, stretched upon forked sticks, and hung up to dry.

Our heroes remained in camp for ten or twelve days, and each morning brought them a fine supply of fur. They met with no other adventure worthy to be related, and one day was like another. They awakened each morning with the sun, and ate their breakfast of broiled venison, fish, or quail, with now and then a rabbit. Upon one occasion they had the breast of a wild turkey. They sought the traps, took the game, prepared the pelts, ate their dinners and suppers of broiled meats and baked sweet potatoes, and slumbered cozily beneath their warm bearskins till morning.

One day Balser noticed that the snow was melting and was falling from the trees. He and his companions had taken enough pelts to make a heavy load upon each of the sleds. They feared that the weather might suddenly grow warm and that the snow might disappear. So they leisurely packed the pelts and their belongings, and next morning started for home on Blue River, the richest, happiest boys in the settlement.

They were glad to go home, but it was with a touch of sadness, when they passed around the bend in the creek, that they said " Good-by " to their " Castle on Brandy- wine."

Printed in the United States of America.